Owned

Book One

The Billionaire Banker Series

Georgia Le Carre

IMPORTANT NOTICE

This book was previously titled
The Billionaire Banker
It is Book 1 of The Billionaire Banker series.
Due to **READER DEMAND** it has been
rewritten in the **First Person POV.**
Do **NOT** purchase this book if you have
already read
The Billionaire Banker.

Table of Contents

Editor:
http://www.loriheaford.com/
Proofreader:
http://nicolarhead.wix.com/proofreadingservices

OWNED

Book 1 of The Billionaire Banker series

Published by Georgia Le Carre

ISBN: 978-1500537098

You can discover more information about Georgia Le Carre and future releases here.

https://www.facebook.com/georgia.lecarre
https://twitter.com/georgiaLeCarre
http://www.goodreads.com/GeorgiaLeCarre

Dedicated to all who have love and passion in their lives,

and to those who are still searching…

You aren't wealthy until you have something money can't buy.

—Garth Brooks

One

Blake Law Barrington

I drop a cube of sugar into the creamy face of my espresso, stir it, and glance at my platinum Greubel

Forsey Tourbillion, acquired at Christie's Important Watches auction last autumn for a cool half a million dollars.

Eight minutes past eight.

I have a party to go to tonight, but I'm giving it a miss. It's been a long day, I am tired, I have to be in New York early tomorrow morning, and it will be one of those incomprehensibly dreary affairs. I take a sip—superb coffee—and return the tiny cup to its white rim.

Summoning a waiter for the check, I sense the activity level in the room take a sudden hike. Automatically, I lift my eyes to where all the other eyes, mostly male and devouring, have veered to. Of course. A girl. In a cheap, orange dress and lap dancer's six-inch high plastic platforms.

You're looking for love in all the wrong places, honey.

A waiter in a burgundy waistcoat bearing the bill has silently materialized at my side. Not taking my eyes off the girl—despite the impossible shoes she has a good walk, sexy—I order myself a whiskey. The waiter slinks away after a right-away-sir nod, and I lean back into the plush chair to watch the show.

It is one of those swanky restaurants where there are transparent black voile curtains hung between the tables and discreet fans to tease and agitate the gauzy material. Three curtains away she stands, minus the shoes, perhaps five feet five or six inches tall. She has the same body type as Lady Gaga, girlishly narrow with fine delicate limbs. Her skin is the color of thick cream. Beautiful mouth. My eyes travel from the waist-length curtain of jet-black hair to the swelling curve of her breasts and hips, and down her shapely legs.

Very nice, but…

At twenty-nine, I am already jaded. Though I watch her with the same speculation of all the other men in the room she is a toy that no longer holds any real excitement for me. I do not need to meet her to *know* her. I have had hundreds like her—hot, greedy pussies and cold, cold hearts. It is always the same. Each one hiding talons of steely ambition that hook into my flesh minutes after they rise like resurrected phoenixes from a night in my bed. Safe to say I have realized the error of my ways.

Still….

Something about her *has* aroused my attention.

She comes further into the room and even the billowing layers of curtains cannot conceal her great beauty or youth. Certainly she is far too young for her dining companion who has just barged in with all the grace of a retired rugby player. I recognize his swollen head instantly. Rupert Lothian. An over-privileged, nerve gratingly colossal ass. He is one of the bank's high profile private customers. The bank never does business with anyone they do not check out first and his report was sickening.

Curious. What could someone so fresh-faced and beautiful be doing with one so noted for ugly games? And they are ugly games that Lothian plays.

I watch three waiters head off towards them and the fluid, elegantly choreographed dance they perform to seat and hand them their menus. Now I have her only in profile. She has put the menu on the table and is sitting ramrod-straight with her hands tightly clasped in her lap. She crosses and uncrosses her legs nervously.

Unbidden, an image pops into my head. It is as alive and wicked as only an image can be. Those long, fine legs entangled in silky sheets. I stare helplessly as she pulls away the sheets, turns that fabulous mouth into a red O, and deliberately opens her legs to expose her sex to me. I see it clearly. A juicy, swollen fruit that my tongue wants to explore! I sit forward abruptly.

Fuck.

I thought I had passed the season of fantasizing about having sex with strangers. I reach for my whiskey and shoot it. From the corner of my eyes I see a waiter discreetly whisper something to Lothian. He rises with all the pomposity he can muster and leaves with the waiter.

I transfer my attention to the girl again. She has collapsed backwards into the chair. Her shoulders sag and her relief is obvious. She stares moodily at the tablecloth, fiddles with her purse and frowns. Then, she seems to visibly force herself away from whatever thoughts troubled her, and lets her glance wander idly around the room until her truly spectacular eyes—I have never seen anything like them before—collide with my unwavering stare. And through the gently shifting black gauze my breath is suddenly punched out of my body, and I am seized by an unthinking, irresistible call to hunt. To possess.

To *own* her.

Two

Lana Bloom

It can have been only seconds, but it seems like ages that I am held locked and hypnotized by the stranger's insolent eyes. When I recall it later I will remember how startlingly white his shirt had been against his tanned throat, and swear that even the air between us had shimmered. Strange too how all the background sounds of cutlery, voices and laughter had faded into nothing. It was as if I had wandered into a strange and compelling universe where there was no one else but me and that devilishly handsome man.

But in this universe I am prey.

The powerful spell is broken when he raises his glass in an ironic salute. Hurriedly, I tear my gaze away, but my thin façade of poise is completely shattered. Hot blood is rushing up into my neck and cheeks; and my heart is racing like a mad thing.

What the hell just happened?

I can still feel his gaze like a burning tingle on my skin. To hide, I bend my head and let my hair fall forward. But the desire to dare another look is so immense it shocks me. I have never experienced such an instant and physical attraction before.

With broad shoulders, a deep tan, smoldering eyes, a strong jaw, and straight-out-of-bed, vogue-cool, catwalk hair that flops onto his forehead, he looks like one of those totally hot and brooding Abercrombie and Fitch models, only more savage and fierce.

Devastatingly more.

But I am not here to flirt with drop dead gorgeous strangers, or to find a man for myself. I press my fingers against my flaming cheeks, and force myself to calm down. All my concentration must go into getting Rupert to agree to my proposal. He is my last hope.

My only hope.

Nothing could ever be more important than my reason for being there with such a man as him. I look miserably towards the tall doors where he has gone. This cold, pillared place of opulence is where rich people come to eat. A waiter wearing white gloves comes through the doors bearing a covered tray. I feel out of my depth. The orange dress is itchy and prickly and I long to scratch several places on my body. Then there are the butterflies flapping dementedly inside my stomach.

Don't ruin this, I tell myself angrily. You've come this far. Nervously, to regain my composure, I press my lips together and firmly push the sarcastically curving mouth out of my mind. I must concentrate on the horrible task ahead. But those insolent eyes, they will not go. So I bring to mind my mother's thin, sad face, and suddenly the stranger's eyes are magically gone. I straighten my back. Prepare myself.

I will not fail.

Rupert, having met whomever he had gone to meet, is weaving his way back to me and when our eyes touch I flash him a brilliant smile. I will not fail. He smiles back triumphantly, and coming around to my side drops me a quick kiss, before slumping heavily into his seat. I have to stop myself from reaching up to wipe my mouth.

I stare at him. He seems transformed. Expansive, almost jolly.

'That's one deal that came in the nick of time. As if the heavens have decided that I deserve you.' The way he says it almost makes me flinch with horror.

'Lucky me,' I say softly, flirtatiously, surprising myself. I tell myself I am playing a part. One that I can vanish into and emerge from unscathed, but I know it is not true. There will be repercussions and consequences.

He smiles nastily. He knows I do not fancy him, but that is part of the thrill. Taking what does not want to be taken.

'Well then,' he says. 'Don't be coy, let's hear it. How much are you going to cost me?'

I take a deep breath. A bull this large can only be taken by the horns. 'Fifty thousand pounds.'

His dirty blond eyebrows shoot upwards, but his voice is mild. 'Not exactly cheap.' His lips thin. 'What do I get for my money?'

We are both startled out of our conversation by a deep, curt voice.

'Rupert.'

'Mr. Barrington,' Rupert gasps, and literally flies to his feet. 'What an unexpected pleasure,' he croons obsequiously. I drop my head with searing shame. It is the stranger. He has heard me sell myself.

'I don't believe I've had the pleasure of your companion's acquaintance,' he says. His voice is an intriguing combination of velvet and husk.

'Blake Law Barrington, Lana Bloom, Lana Bloom, Blake Law Barrington.'

I look up then, a long way up—he is definitely over six feet, maybe six two or three—to meet his stormy-gray stare. I search them for disgust, but they are carefully veiled, impenetrable pits of mystery. Perhaps, he has not heard me sell myself, after all. I begin to tremble. My body knows something I do not. He is dangerous to me in a way I cannot yet conceive.

'Hello, Lana.'

'Hi,' I reply. My voice sounds tiny. Like a child that has been told to greet an adult.

He puts his hand out, and after a perceptible hesitation, I put mine into it. His hand is large and warm, and his clasp firm and safe, but I snatch mine away as if burnt. He breaks his gaze briefly to glance at Rupert.

'There is a party tonight at Lord Jakie's,' he says before those darkly fringed eyes return to me again. Inscrutable as ever. 'Would you like to come as my guests?' It is as if he is addressing only me. It sends delicious shivers up and down my spine. Confused, by the unfamiliar sensations I tear my eyes away from him and look at Rupert.

Rupert's eyebrows are almost in his hairline. 'Lord Jakie?' he repeats. There is unconcealed delight in his face. He seems a man who has found a bottle of rare wine in his own humble cellar. 'That's terribly kind of you, Mr. Barrington. Terribly kind. Of course, we'd love to,' he accepts for both of us.

'Good. I'll leave your names at the door. See you there.' He nods at me and I register the impression that he is obsessively clean and controlled. There is no mess in this man's life. A place for everything and everything in its place. Then he is gone.

Rupert and I watch him walk away. He has the stride of a supremely confident man. Rupert turns to face me again; his face is mean and at odds to his words. 'Well, well,' he drawls, 'You must be my lucky charm.'

'Why?'

'First, I get the deal I've been after for the last year and a half, then the great man not only deigns to speak to me, but invites me to a party thrown by the crème de la crème of high society.'

'Who is he?'

'He, my dear, is the next generation of arguably the richest family in the world.'

'*The* Barringtons?' I whisper, shocked.

'He even smells of old money and establishment, doesn't he?' Rupert says, and neighs loudly at his own joke. Rupert himself smells like grated lemon peel. The citrusy scent reminds me of Fairy washing up liquid.

A waiter appears to ask what we would like to drink.

'We'll have your finest house champagne,' Rupert booms. He winks at me. 'We're celebrating.'

A bottle and ice bucket arrive with flourish. The only time I have drunk champagne is when Billie and I dressed up to the nines and presented ourselves as bride and bridesmaid to be, at the Ritz. We pretended I was about to drop forty thousand pounds into their coffers by cutting my wedding cake there. We quaffed half a bottle of champagne and a whole tray of canapés while being shown around the different function rooms. Afterwards, Billie thanked them nicely and said we would be in touch. How we had laughed on the bus journey back.

I watch as the waiter expertly extracts the cork with a quiet hiss. Another waiter in a black jacket reels off the specials for the night and asks us if we are ready to order.

Rupert looks at me. 'The beef on the bone here is very good.'

I smile weakly. 'I guess I'll just have whatever you're having.'

'I'm actually having steak tartare.'

'Then I'll have the same.'

He looks at the waiter. 'A dozen oysters to start then steak tartare and side orders of vegetables and mashed potatoes.'

'I'm not really hungry. No starter for me,' I say quickly.

When the waiter is gone, he raises his glass. 'To us.'

'To us,' I repeat softly. The words stick in my throat.

I take a small sip and taste nothing, so I put the glass on the table and look at my hands blankly. I have to find something interesting to say.

'You have very beautiful skin,' he says softly. 'It was the first thing I noticed about you. Does it…mark very easily?'

'Yes,' I admit warily.

'I knew it,' he boasts with a sniff. 'I am a connoisseur of skin. I love the taste and the touch of skin. I can already imagine the taste of yours. A skin of wine.' He eyes me greedily over the rim of his glass.

I have been trying my best not to look at the dandruff flakes that liberally dust the shoulders of his pin-striped suit, but with that last remark he has tossed his head and a flurry of motes have floated off his head and fallen onto the pristine tablecloth. My eyes have helplessly followed their progress. I look up to find him looking at me speculatively.

'What will I be getting for my money?' His voice is suddenly cold and hard.

I blink. It is all wrong. I shouldn't be here. In this dress, or shoes, sitting in front of this obscene piece of filth hiding behind his handmade shirt, gold cufflinks and plummy, upper class accent. This man degrades and offends me simply by looking at me. I wish myself somewhere else, but I am here. All my credit cards are maxed out. Two banks have impolitely turned me down and there is nothing else to do, but be here in this dress and these slutty shoes…

My stomach in knots, I smile in what I hope is a seductive way. 'What would you like for your money?'

'Forget what I would like for the moment. What are you selling?' His eyes are spiteful in a way I cannot understand.

'Me, I guess.'

That makes him snort with cruel laughter. 'You are an extraordinarily beautiful girl, but to be honest I can get five first class supermodels right off the runway for that asking price. What makes you think you're worth that kind of money?'

I take a deep breath. Here goes. 'I'm a virgin.'

He stops laughing. A suspicious speculative look enters his pale blue eyes. 'How old are you?'

'Twenty.' Well, I will be in two months' time.

He frowns. 'And you say you're still a virgin?'

'Yes.'

‘Saving yourself up for someone special, were you?’ His tone is annoying.

‘Does it matter?’ My nails bite into my clenched fists.

His eyes glitter. ‘No, I suppose not.’ He pauses. ‘How do I know you’re not lying?’

I swallow hard. The taste of my humiliation is bitter. ‘I’ll undergo any medical tests you require me to.’

He laughs. ‘No need. No need,’ he dismisses genially. ‘Blood on the sheets will be enough for me.’

The way he says blood makes my blood run cold.

‘Are all orifices up for sale?’

Oh! the brutality of the man. Something dies inside me, but I keep the image of my mother in my mind, and my voice is clear and strong. ‘Yes.’

‘So all that is left is to renegotiate the price?’

I have to stop myself from recoiling. I know now that I have committed two out of the nine sorts of behaviors my mother has warned me are considered contemptible and base. I have expected generosity from a miser and I have revealed my need to my enemy. ‘The price is not negotiable.’

His gaze sweeps meaningfully to my champagne glass. ‘Shall we give this party a go first and bargain later, when you are in a…better mood?’

I understand his thinking. He thinks he can drive the price down when I am drunk. ‘The price is not negotiable,’ I say firmly. ‘And will have to be paid up front.’

He smiles smarmily. ‘I’m sure we’ll come to some agreement that we will both be happy with.’

I frown. I have been naïve. My plan is sketchy and has no provisions for a sharp punter or price negotiations. I heard through the office grapevine where I worked as temporary secretary that my boss was one of those men who are prepared to pay ten thousand pounds a pop for his pleasure and often, but I had never imagined he would reduce me to bargaining.

While Rupert stuffs himself with cheese and biscuits I excuse myself and go to the Ladies. There is another woman standing at the mirror. She glances at me with a mixture of surprise and disgust. I wait until she leaves, then I call my mother.

'Hi, Mum.'

'Where are you, Lana?'

'I'm still at the restaurant.'

'What time will you be coming home?'

'I'll be late. I've been invited to a party.'

'A party,' my mother repeats worriedly. 'Where?'

'I don't know the address. Somewhere in London.'

'How will you get home?' A wire of panic has crept into her voice.

I sigh gently. I have almost never left my mother alone at night; consequently she is now a bundle of jittery nerves. 'I have a ride, Mum. Just don't wait up for me, OK?'

'All right. Be careful, won't you?'

'Nothing is going to happen to me.'

'Yes, yes,' she says, but she sounds distracted and unhappy.

'How are you feeling, Mum?'

'Good.'

'Goodnight, then. I'll see you in the morning.'

'Lana?'

'Yeah.'

'I love you very much.'

'Me too, Mum. Me too.'

I flip my phone shut with a snap. I no longer feel cheap or obscene, but strong and sure. There is nothing Rupert can do that can degrade me. I will have that money no matter what.

I look at myself in the mirror. No need for lipstick as I have hardly eaten—just watching Rupert gurgle down the oysters made me feel quite sick, and how was I to know steak tartare was ground raw meat. For a moment I think again of that sinfully sophisticated man, his eyes edged with experience and mystery, his lips twisted with sensuality, and I am suddenly overcome by a strong desire to press my body against his hard length. But he is gone and I am here.

I return my phone to my purse and go out to meet my fate.

Three

'Shall we go?' Rupert asks, and before I can agree, he imperiously clicks his fingers for the bill. Outside, Rupert hails a black cab. It is such a warm evening that I carry my coat in my hands. Rupert gives the address to the cab driver and we climb in. My dress rides up my thighs, and when I try to pull it back down, Rupert puts his meaty, white hand over mine and in a firm voice orders, 'Leave it.'

Embarrassed, I look into the rearview mirror. The taxi driver is observing us. Wordlessly, I drape my coat over my exposed thighs and knees and turning my face away from Rupert, stare out. Damn him. As I gaze unseeingly out I feel his hand slide under my coat and settle on my thighs. Biting my lip I try to ignore the hand, but it is steadily slithering upwards. When it is almost at my crotch I catch the offending hand in a firm grip. I turn to him and look him in the eye.

'We don't have a deal yet.'

'True,' he says in a mild and reasonable way, and retracts his hand, but the smile on his face is taunting and smug. He has already figured out that I need the money desperately and my body is my last option.

The rest of the journey passes in silence while my stomach churns. I am so nervous I actually worry I will lose the few vegetables I did eat on the floor of the cab. Fortunately, the taxi turns into Bishop's Avenue and we come to a stop outside a large, white, three-story Regency house. There are fancy cars parked bumper to bumper along the length of the street.

Rupert pays the cab driver and we walk up a short flight of steps to a set of black doors. Rupert rings the bell and through the tall windows I get a glimpse of the kind of people that I have only seen in magazines: immaculately dressed and dripping in jewelry. I look down upon my cheap orange dress in dismay. I try to pull at the hem, but my efforts at modesty are counter-productive, as more of my cleavage falls into view.

'Don't worry,' Rupert lies cheerfully. 'You'll do.'

A round man in an old-fashioned butler's uniform opens the door. His manner suggests disdain. He can tell instantly we do not belong. Rupert haughtily informs him that we are guests of Blake Barrington. The man's eyes register recognition and a glimmer of a smile surfaces. He nods politely and stands aside to allow us in. I fill my lungs with as much oxygen as I can and enter the grand hallway. Inside I stifle a gasp at my splendid surroundings.

From outside it had not appeared so large and spacious. Now I understand what Rupert meant by the smell of old money. I have never been anywhere so beautiful. The walls are covered with museum quality paintings. I gaze up with awe at the cherubs and Madonna-like women looking down at me. They are so beautiful that I want a closer look, but Rupert is guiding me firmly by the elbow towards a sort of anteroom where a young woman takes my coat in exchange for a ticket.

From two open doorways live classical music and voices emanate. A waiter carrying a tray of champagne stops in front of us. I hardly drunk at the restaurant in an effort to remain sober and level-headed, but now I know I must be drunk or I will never be able to go through my deal with the devil. A pasty white devil with dandruff.

I take a glass, and with a restraining hand on the surprised waiter's arm, drain the tall flute. The bubbles hit me at the back of my throat and make my eyes water. I return the empty glass to the tray and snag another two.

'Thanks,' I say breathlessly, and the waiter, a young Mediterranean type, allows his dark, restless eyes to wander down to my chest.

Rupert watches me with feral, excited eyes. He wants me drunk. He has plans for me. By the small of my back he guides me into one of the rooms. Surreptitiously, I note the other women's clothes. Classy, understated and expensive, very expensive.

I feel many pairs of eyes on me and it is impossible not to be aware that I stand out like a sore thumb. I turn resolutely away from their openly condescending gazes and look towards the string quartet only to find their eyes on me too. Damn that Barrington guy for inviting us here. Defiantly, I suck my champagne glass dry. Another waiter passes and I pull another glass from the tray.

'Go easy,' Rupert warns.

I turn towards him with a bright smile. 'I thought you wanted me drunk and pliable.'

He takes my elbow and leads me deeper into the room close to a large palm plant. With his back to the party he says, 'I don't like fucking inert bodies.'

My eyes widen. Still the champagne must have already gone to my head for I feel inordinately courageous. I'm ready to talk terms with him. 'Right, you don't want inert bodies. What do you want, Rupert?'

From the camel's lips came cold breath. 'Have you read *Fifty Shades Of Grey*?'

Almost all the other girls at the agency have read the book and I have been present while they have raved about it, but I have been confused by its popularity. Did women really have a secret desire to be *owned* by a powerful man? Could it be love when a man wants to tie you up and flog you raw? When I mentioned it to my mother, she smiled and astutely remarked, 'The Western woman sneered at the woman in the purdah and now she dons a dog collar and worships at the same altar.'

I look into Rupert's pale eyes. 'No, but isn't it about a sick man who abuses his lover?'

'Perhaps it is not a sickness, but a matter of taste.'

'Is that what you want from me?'

'Not quite. What I really like is taking a woman by force. A dangerous activity likely to end me behind bars, so I am willing to settle for consensual rape. You will meet me in parks and alleyways, or I will pick you up in my car from a street corner and you will pretend to resist while I overpower you and rape you. There will be a bit of pain and sometimes it will involve a little bleeding, but I will never mark your face or leave any permanent scars. And when I am finished I will leave you in the gutter to make your own way back. Would that be acceptable to you?'

Shocked to my core, I hear my own voice as if from far away ask, 'How many times would you expect this… service from me?'

'Let's say five times?' Rupert's face freezes into a cold, calculating mask. A businessman to the end. Ten thousand must be the going price.

I feel as if I am a stick-figured bird precariously perched on a thin wire. Can I really agree to let someone rape me? Even with all the champagne sloshing inside me I find I am unable to speak. I nod.

'Perhaps I should let you lick the brim to taste the poison,' he murmurs, and moves closer to me. Instinctively, I take a step back on my tall shoes, and if not for the solid wall against my back, I would have fallen. With the trailing fronds of a palm tree and his big body hiding me from the party his hand comes up to pinch my right nipple. So hard I gasp in shock and pain.

He takes that opportunity to crash down on my parted mouth, bumps his teeth against my lips, and pokes a pointy, muscular tongue into my mouth. His tongue tastes coppery and bitter.

Copious amounts of saliva pour into my horrified mouth making me want to gag. The oysters I have not eaten but watched him eat flash into my mind. His tongue feels slimy and dirty. It makes me want to brush my teeth, rinse, spit, and rinse again with the extra-strong mouthwash that my father used to have in the bathroom cabinet. I truly, truly need to go somewhere and be sick, but pinned tightly to the wall by his strong ox-like body I am totally unable to move.

I feel his hand force itself between my thighs and slide up quickly. His rough, sausage-like fingers are already grasping the rim of my knickers and pushing the material aside. And there is not a single thing I can do about it. Helpless tears gather at the backs of my eyes and begin to roll down my face.

Suddenly he removes his smelly mouth and looks down at me. My face, I am certain, must be white with horror and I am gasping for breath. My distress seems to please him and my suffering appears to have brought him pleasure. Without knowing it I am playing the part perfectly. If I had enjoyed it, it would have spoilt it for him.

He brings up a hand and touches my face. 'For most part the symptoms of excitement and fear are so similar most men cannot tell the difference. I can,' he whispers close to my ear, the thick fingers of his other hand moving into the folds of my flesh. 'I am going to finger-fuck you amongst all these high and mighty people and none of them will ever know.'

At that moment I am filled with an unspeakable loathing for him. My brain scrambles for escape. 'Don't you care,' I whisper back, 'what these people will think of us? Of you? I thought you were pleased to be in the company of the crème de la crème of society.'

His laugh is harsh and sudden. 'Did you see anybody come to greet me or talk to me? I am as invisible as you are, probably more so. Nobody is looking at us, because nobody cares about us. We are the outsiders.'

Desperately, I push the palms of my hands against his chest. The nausea is already almost in my throat. I must be sick. 'I need the toilet,' I gasp.

He hesitates for a second and then he smiles. It is the smile of a man who is too pleased with himself. 'It's not very posh to say toilet. This lot call it the loo. Go on, then,' he says, and steps aside.

The first thing my shocked, ashamed eyes meet is Blake. There is a blonde in a long red dress wrapped around him, but he is staring at me with an expression on his face I cannot fathom. His eyes are blazing.

For a moment I stare back. Then I snap my mouth shut, tear my eyes from his, and pushing myself away from the wall take a step forward. My knees feel shaky and I am terrified I will fall, but I do not. I just need to get away. Away from the scene of my humiliation. I sense heads turning to watch me, disgusted expressions and haughty whispers. I stumble away towards the doors hardly able to control the rising nausea.

I don't dare open my mouth to ask anyone where the loos are, but I spot two young women disappearing down a corridor and I stagger after them. They lead me to a cloakroom and I rudely push past them, ignoring their offended cries of 'Hey'. I run into one of two cubicles and falling to my knees violently throw up the bits of vegetables I have eaten and almost all the champagne. One of the girls asks if I am all right and I choke out, 'Fine'.

I hear them go into the other cubicle and lock the door.

I sit back on my heels and the hot tears come. I cover my mouth to muffle any stray sounds. I have made a complete fool of myself. What do I do now? What can I do? Numbly I hear the girls in the next cubicle giggling about what all girls giggle and chat about—men. Then my ears pick up the sounds of them snorting lines of cocaine. When they leave I flush the toilet and open the door.

Miserably, I walk towards the very large ornate, gilded mirror stretched across the wall. The other toilet seems to be in use and a thin woman with immaculate hair is perched on one of the gold and cream chairs waiting her turn. There is an air of superior calm about her. Her eyes meet mine briefly but curiously, before she enters the cubicle that I have vacated.

I stare at myself in the mirror. My face is deathly pale and the cheap mascara I purchased from the market is smudged and running; my lips look as if I have smacked my mouth on a wall, and my eyes are red and puffy from crying. *This is what Blake Barrington saw*. I look like I feel. Soiled.

The woman in the other cubicle comes out. She looks identical to the woman who had perched on the chair before. With a quick, surprised glance at me, she goes to stand at the other end of the mirror. She pats her immaculate hair, brushes away imaginary specks of dust from her soft pink dress suit and leaves.

I turn on the tap and rinse my mouth with plenty of water. Scooping water in my palms I wash my face with hand soap and scrub it dry with a paper towel. Without my make-up I feel defenseless and naked. But I'm not going to try and put lipstick on these swollen lips.

I hunker down and weigh my situation.

There is a sick pervert out there who wants to rape me and leave me torn and bleeding in alleyways. Five times. *I could walk away. Say fuck you.* Actually, no I can't. It is so much money. And he knows it. I *need* that money. I consider taking the money and not delivering. What could he do? It's not like he could go to the police or I would be running a refund desk. Then I remember his eyes. How cold and dangerous. No. Anyway, I have always said, I'd rather be the one who bought the Brooklyn Bridge than the one who sold it.

Again my thoughts turn to the Barrington man. Why is he still in my mind? Probably the way he looks at me. No one. Absolutely no one has looked at me like that.

I indulge in a moment of fantasy. Perhaps he really wants me. He is filthy rich so he will simply give me the money I need. Gallantly, he will then fall in love with me and we will marry. As I am standing inside my dreams another woman opens the door and enters. It is the blonde in the red dress. She is tall and severely beautiful with an aristocratic nose and bottle-green eyes. She has the same superior air of all the people at this party. The same air that Blake Barrington has claimed for himself.

I cannot help but watch her through the mirror. Our eyes meet for a second, then hers slide away, but in that second there is pure speculation. Everybody knows I do not belong.

I look at my reflection. Who am I kidding? Blake Barrington is the biggest cheese on the board. Simply the way Rupert behaved in his presence told me that. He was probably looking at me because I am dressed like a hooker and he thinks I am one. The only real thing I have is my mother. And there is nothing I will not do for her. I think of my father. How easily he had walked away when we had needed him most. How weak his love for us had been. Mine is different. I will not walk away even if I have to walk upon a path of thorns. Bleed in alleyways I will. And that will be the test of my love.

I will not let myself be distracted by anything. I will survive any sexual humiliation Rupert can dish out. Five encounters? My champagne-addled brain scoffs, that's fucking nothing. The beautiful blonde has turned away from the mirror and entered one of the cubicles.

Blake Barrington is welcome to her.

I straighten my spine. I can do this, I tell my reflection. I love you, Mum, better than Dad did, much, much better. I practice the smile I will bestow on Rupert in the mirror, and despite the revulsion in my belly I tell myself that when I am old and wrinkled I will be glad I made this sacrifice. The price will always be worth it. Then there is nothing left to do in that opulent loo, but to walk out of it, and face my decision, and the lengths I will go to for my mother.

I open the door and my heart drops.

Blake Barrington is lounging casually against the wall of the corridor.

Four

He straightens when he sees me. He looks annoyed. Perhaps, he is pissed off that he invited Rupert and me to his mate's fine party, and we've showed him up and behaved in a disgusting manner. But, quite frankly, I didn't ask to be invited. The very last thing I need is another confrontation. I have quite enough on my plate. I consider ignoring him and walking right past but he raises a detaining finger. I look defiantly up at him. Thank God, for my shoes. They lift my eyes to the level of his straight, stern mouth.

His eyes scan my face, now devoid of all make-up. 'Are you all right?'

Up this close his skin is sun kissed and his voice pure velvet. I fold my arms around my body and resist the instinct to take a step back, such is the immensity of animal power he exudes. It is magnetic and irresistible. It's trite I know but he reminds me of a caged panther. Prowling and ready to pounce, full of suppressed restless energy. Muscular, strong.

I raise my chin, meet him square in the eye, and in my best secretarial voice, say, 'Yes, I'm fine. Thank you.'

'I need to talk to you.'

Oh God, he is going to lecture me. 'So talk.'

'Privately—through here, please.' He gestures with his hand, and is careful not to touch me. The corridor leads to a door. He goes ahead of me and holds it open. I hesitate for a moment, then think, fuck it, I'm not scared of you, and walk through. The room appears to be some sort of library with walls full of shelves filled with leather-bound books. It smells of wood polish and tobacco. I hear him close the door and turn around to face him.

He is leaning against the door and simply watching me.

'Well?' I prompt.

'Are you over eighteen?'

'Yes.'

'Are you sure?'

'Of course I am,' I snap. 'Not that it is any of your business.'

'What will Lothian get for his money?'

So he *did* hear. Oh the shame. If the ground could have opened up and swallowed me… Fortunately, a fine anger comes to my rescue. How dare he? The audacity. Overbearing, arrogant bastard. With all the hauteur I can manage under the circumstances, I grate, 'That's private if you don't mind, and if that was all…'

'It's not idle curiosity. I'm quite happy to double the sum if it's what I think it is.'

I stare at him blankly. I can understand why someone like Rupert would have to pay, but Blake Law Barrington? He could have anyone he wants. Then it occurs to me that, perhaps, he is just toying with me. Perhaps it is a thing all rich men do.

My pride comes to the fore. I will not be humiliated twice in one night. 'Whatever I have offered is for Rupert and Rupert only. Now please get away from that door and the hell away from me.' My voice has risen in anger.

His eyes spark. 'Do you know your eyes are like the blue of struck matches when you are angry.' Then more softly, 'Why would anyone, let alone a stunner like you, get involved with someone who, if the most impeccable sources are to be trusted, is an absolute brute? He beat one woman so badly he broke her jaw, and blinded her in one eye.'

I have drunk too much champagne. The whole situation has become impossible for me to deal with in my present condition. I have ventured where I should never have gone. I feel the sting of defeat in mybones. 'What do you want from me?'

He leaves the door and walks towards me: again that sensation that he is a predatory animal. 'Well for a start…' He reaches me and suddenly jerks me towards him. I fall forward and am pitched against the unyielding hardness of his body. My palms come into contact with the smooth material of his jacket. Shocked, I am filled with the scent that Rupert called old money and establishment. Difficult to define, but it reminds me of rosemary, not because of its smell, but because it is so clear and distinct. Nothing wishy-washy about it.

Everything takes on an unreal appearance. The fabulously wealthy interior. The man outside that door that wants to rape me for money. The frighteningly remote man in front of me that brings into my body sensations I have never experienced before. A pulse at the base of his throat is throbbing. I watch it curiously. I have never seen it in a man before.

And then an arm comes around me, a fistful of hair close to my nape is grasped and tugged so my confused face is tilted up towards him. 'This,' he says and his mouth swoops down to possess mine. His breath smells like brandy or whiskey. Wicked, anyway.

Twice today I have had to endure a stranger's uninvited and unwelcome lips, but my reaction to this overbearing man is shocking and immediate.

His mouth drives me wild in a way that I could never have imagined. Heat ripples through me, and the reasoning, reliable part of my brain, that part that has never failed me before, stops responding. Stops functioning. My arms snake up to twine around his neck and tangle in the thick hair. I thrill in his possessive hold.

He circles my tongue, sucks it deep into his mouth and kisses me with such ferocity that some slumbering beast inside answers his animal call. A dangerous excitement kicks hard in the pit of my belly. No man has ever done this to me in this way before. I cling to him. Like a blind animal that moves only with instinct I push my body into his. There is only the need to find more of such addictive heat. What I find is the thick hardness of his desire for me. It presses aggressively against the softness of my stomach and excites me beyond all reason.

A pleasure that is at once sweet and piercing courses through my body. This rock-hard erection is mine. I caused it. Heat pools between my legs. And suddenly I am wet with wanting and filled with an irresistible desire to have that hard meat inside me, as deep as it will go…

I totally forget where I am.

It is Rupert's cold, hard voice that drags me back into that room. We had both not heard him enter. 'I'm afraid she's rather spoken for,' he drawls, but there is so much suppressed anger that his voice is like a blast of icy air.

I snatch my mouth away from Blake's. He is positioned between Rupert and me so his wide chest hides me from Rupert's condemnation and my eyes, cloudy with confusion and desire, are still caught in his gaze. For a few seconds more he does not release me, but simply stares into my eyes with something approaching surprise. Then his eyes turn into hard granite chips and his body stiffens even as his hands tighten and curve protectively around my waist. Slowly he turns to face Rupert.

'But still unpaid for, I believe?' he says, and looks down with a smile at my flushed, troubled face. I have two very quick impressions. He is a brilliant actor and he is a cold man. A shockingly cold and unemotional being.

Rupert directs his astonished, vicious eyes at me. 'You offered yourself to him too?'

I stare mutely at Rupert while his gaze moves derisively, hatefully over me. I feel myself cringe horribly, but I try not to show it.

'Does he know how much you charge?'

One sculptured eyebrow rises gently. 'Do you doubt I will be able to afford her?'

Rupert shrivels the way a leech that has had salt thrown on it does. 'This is why you invited me here, isn't it?'

'Yes.'

'What a joke!' he taunts, but his jibe lacks any real bite. 'The great Barrington can't find his own whore. He has to steal mine.'

'I didn't steal her,' Blake notes reasonably. 'I just offered to pay more.'

Rupert's eyes bulge, bug-like. 'She's just a cheap bloody tart. I've just finger-fucked her out there,' he lies maliciously, jerking his dandruff-laden head in the direction of the door.

I feel Blake's hand tighten around my waist. 'Consider it an unearned freebie, then,' he says quietly, but there is warning in the calm words. A warning that is not lost on Rupert. The air becomes tight with tension. I look from one man to the other. It is like watching two lions fighting for supremacy. But my body knows which lion it wants to win this fight.

Rupert shrugs. He knows he'd be a fool to go against a Barrington. He has much to lose. 'If you think I'm going to fight over her you're mistaken. Have her.'

He turns on his heel and leaves.

Blake lets go of me and I realize I am trembling. I lean against the desk, hating myself, but unable to stop —nothing is more important than the money—I ask, 'Did you…did you mean it about the money?'

'Yes.'

A sob of relief escapes my throat. I cover my mouth with both hands. 'Thank you.'

He looks at me with narrowed eyes, as if surprised by the intensity of my reaction, but he does not offer any comment. 'Did you have a coat?'

I nod, unable to speak.

'Give me the ticket. I'll get it.'

I rummage through the purse hanging by my hips, my hands unsteady, and shake my head glumly. For the life of me I cannot remember what I have done with it. 'I've lost it. I think it might have fallen out in the…' I am about to say loo when I decide I am not like them and I won't pretend to be something I am not… 'Ladies room.'

'Let's go. I'll buy you another.'

'I can't leave without it. It's not mine,' I whisper.

He sighs. 'It's all right. I'll get it. Is the coat…er… orange?'

I look at him carefully—there is an insult there, somewhere—but his face is blank. 'Yes.'

'Wait here. Don't go anywhere.'

I stand in the middle of the room feeling light-headed. I've got the money and I don't have to get raped for it. My hands find their way to my mouth. That kiss. The way it made me feel. Just thinking about it makes me long for the feel of his solid body melded into mine.

The door opens, and oh shit—Rupert walks in.

'You look frightened. Why? I don't wish you harm. In fact, I realize now that I am actually very interested in your offer. If I seemed unappreciative before please forgive me.'

'There is,' I say, shaking my head and taking a step backwards, 'nothing to forgive.'

'Is he really paying double?'

'I don't need more than what I asked you for.'

'Then why go to him? He is no different from me. He will drop you like a bad mortgage when he is finished with you too.'

I nod. 'Of course he will, but like you said, I came with a price. You wanted to bargain and he was willing to pay it.' If only I can keep him talking until Blake returns.

'So am I, now.'

'Besides, you want fifty shades of gray and he just wants a woman.'

'Perhaps I've changed my mind. Perhaps I just want a woman too.'

He comes closer.

'Blake has gone to get my coat. He'll be back any time.'

'Not without this he won't.' He holds out my ticket.

He puts out a hand suddenly. I try to move back, but he grabs me by the arm, his grip vice-like, his fingers digging painfully into my flesh. He hauls me closer.

'You're hurting me.'

'You'll be surprised how much pain the human body can take.'

'What do you want, Rupert?'

'I feel aggrieved. Something I wanted and was promised to me has been stolen by another. I was given a taste of something, which I very much liked. You resist beautifully, Lana. Perhaps, you will do both of us. I will pay you too.'

I blink. I can't believe what I am hearing. If it wasn't so humiliating, it would be surreal. The surroundings I am in, the obviously powerful men who are suddenly apparently willing to pay huge sums to have sex with me.

'I wouldn't do that to Blake.'

'He'll never know and even if he does, he won't care. It's not like he wants to marry you. You're just a fuck, Lana,' he pronounces dismissively.

The door opens and Blake stands at the threshold with my orange coat folded over his arm. His face is like a closed steel door. He comes into the room and Rupert lets go of my arm and I immediately move away from him, rubbing my stinging flesh. Already there are red marks on it. Blake eyes them silently, then helps me into my coat.

'Ready?' he asks.

I nod.

He turns towards Rupert and socks him hard on the chin. So hard the ex-rugby player falls to the floor with a grunt.

'She may be a cheap slut, but I'm paying what you baulked at, so she is my cheap slut now. You'd do well to remember that,' Blake throws casually over his shoulder.

Rupert clutches his busted, bleeding lip and shows his fury to the only person he dares to. 'You're fired, Bloom,' he shouts impotently.

Blake takes my arm and leads me out of that place. There is not a single person at that party that does not turn to watch us leave.

Five

Blake's monster of a car, a gleaming sable-gray Aston Martin is parked beside a lamppost. It is one of those old-fashioned wrought-iron ones with a fluted surface. I stand on the curb and loop my hand around its rough, cold metal.

'Get in,' he says.

'What if I'm sick in your car?'

'My secretary will have it valeted.'

I unhook myself from the metal post. Is life really this easy? With these shoes and the drink in me it is impossible to get into the low-swung seat elegantly. Blake's eyes are on my legs. He is going to be seeing a lot more soon, so I swing the last one in and shut the door.

The interior of his car is plush and luxurious. It even smells expensive. I have never been in such a car. The sound system is excellent and superb music fills the car.

'What is this music called?'

'Handel's *Messiah,*' he says, and switches it off. He turns to me. In the light of the streetlamp he looked harsh and distant. In the softly lit darkness of his car there is still no softening to his face. Again the thought, a cold, cold man.

'I have to be in New York tomorrow, but my secretary will call you and make all the necessary arrangements.'

I nod gratefully and look away. It is as if I am in a dream.

'Where do you live?'

'Kilburn.'

'Got a postcode?' He sounds very American then.

I give it to him and he sets his GPS system.

We drive in silence, until I can bear it no more. 'Don't you want to know how much?'

'Yeah, tell me.'

I tell him and his eyes leave the road briefly to look at me. 'What made you think Rupert was the man for the part?'

I shrug in the dark. 'I don't know. I heard a rumor that his secretary was sometimes tasked with stuffing envelopes with ten thousand pounds in cash and booking pricey hotel rooms for him.'

'I see,' he says quietly.

We come to a red light.

'Why me?' I ask.

His fingers tap at the steering wheel. Long, strong fingers. I stare at them and think of the way they moved on my body. He turns to me. His eyes are edgy and dangerous, full of promise. 'Do you want it flowery or straight.'

I bite my lip. 'Straight.'

'I wanted to fuck you senseless from the moment our eyes met.'

'And the flowery version?'

'Now I think about it, there is no flowery version. It is what it is.'

I turn to look at his profile. It is very stern and still. Have I jumped from the frying pan into the fire? Are all rich people secretly deviant in their sexual desires? 'Does fucking me senseless involve any weird or kinky stuff?'

He glances at me. Again that expression that is beyond my comprehension. 'No, but I want to be able to use you as often as I please in whatever manner I desire for as long as I choose.'

'Oh!' How strange, but his insulting words unleashes a lightning thrill of sexual excitement in my body. 'I… How long were you thinking?'

'I'll decide tomorrow. But I imagine one month should do it.'

'Do it?'

'Get me bored.'

'And you are willing to pay a hundred thousand pounds for that?'

His lips twist into a wry smile. 'When I made my offer I didn't realize you had valued yourself quite that highly, but I'm not displeased that you did. Despite all protestations to the contrary, nobody really wants a bargain. They settle for it because they can't afford better.' He glances at me. 'Cheap usually means get your guard up, you are being offered something undesirable.'

I think of my mother trawling the supermarket aisles looking for stuff that has been discounted because it is reaching the end of its sell by date. 'I will require the money up front. So, how will we do this?'

'My lawyer will draw up the appropriate contract for you to sign. Once you have done so the money will be in your account within minutes.'

'What sort of a contract?'

'A non-disclosure agreement.'

I nod. 'I suppose rich people have to protect themselves.'

'Yes,' he replies shortly.

An awkward silence follows. He seems preoccupied with his own thoughts. I turn my head—it has begun to throb—and look out of the window. He is a fast driver and we are already on Edgware Road.

'I'll send someone around tomorrow at noon to take you to your workplace so you can collect your personal belongings.'

'It's OK, I can go on my own.'

'I'd feel happier if you were accompanied. Indulge me.'

I think for a moment. I don't exactly relish the prospect of accidentally bumping into Rupert either. 'Well, I only have an old pair of trainers there. I won't bother to pick them up.'

'As you wish.'

We arrive at the block of council flats where I live and he looks around him in surprise as if he has never been to such a poor area before.

'You live here?' He cannot hide his distaste. I guess to him it must be a horrible housing estate, what he would probably consider the underbelly of the city.

'Yes,' I say simply.

He stops the car outside a two-story block of flats. 'Which one is yours?'

I point to the last flat on the first floor, and say, 'That's me.'

He doesn't switch off the engine but turns to me. 'Give me your phone.'

I hand it to him.

He punches in some numbers and waits. When his phone rings, he ends the call. 'I've got your number and you've got mine,' he says and hands my phone back to me.

'Thank you.'

'Take a couple of aspirins and go to bed. Keep yourself free tomorrow. The entire day.'

'OK.'

'I'll be in touch tomorrow evening.'

Instead of driving off he sits in his car and watches me totter and wobble in my ridiculously high shoes over to the cemented verge, gain the cracked concrete concourse, and go up an outer staircase while holding onto the metal railings. At the entrance to my home I turn back and flick my wrist to indicate that I am safely home and that he need wait no more. He doesn't respond. Simply sits there. Watching me.

'Fine. Whatever,' I huff to myself. Sitting on the front step, I take off my shoes. With them in my hand I put my key in the door and turn it.

It is only after I close my front door and hear the powerful engine take off that I realize neither man has wanted to know why I need the money. The flat is lit only by the lights from the streetlamps. I walk barefoot into the kitchen and fumble around in the darkness. Finally, I find a tab of paracetamols, punch two out and sit with a glass of water at the kitchen table in a stunned daze. What a night it has been. I set out with an absurd idea and…

'I've done it,' I whisper to the familiar shadows, and grin.

I think of the stone-like biceps and the hard slab of his stomach that my hands and body encountered and I touch my mouth. I can still feel his lips, his hands. I remember how I lost control and totally forgot myself. And the unfamiliar too damn good sensation he caused in my body, between my legs. Is it too dreamlike to be true?

This cannot be just my life.

Don't be too happy yet. He could still change his mind.

I swallow the paracetamols and avoiding all the creaky areas on the stairs tiptoe upstairs. The light is off in my mother's room, so I quietly open the door to look in on her sleeping form. But my mother is sitting on a chair by the window. She must have seen me come in.

'What are you doing?' I ask.

'I heard you come in,' she says softly.

'Could you not sleep?'

'No. I start my chemo next week. Just enjoying the feeling of well-being I guess.'

I cross the room and kneel beside my mother. She is not wearing a scarf, and her bald head glints in the moonlight. It makes me sad. 'I've got good news for you, Mum. Remember that clinic in America that I was telling you about.'

She frowns. She is only fifty but the worry and pain make her appear haggard. 'The one we can't afford.'

'Well, it's not a hundred percent yet, but I think I've managed to raise the money.'

'How? How did you do that?' My mother's voice is suspicious and frightened.

'I met a guy. A rich guy who just wants to help.'

'A rich man who wants to help?' Her tone is frankly disbelieving.

'Mum, please don't be like that. It's not anything like you are thinking.'

'Oh no? What is it like then?'

'He's just a nice guy who likes me.'

'I wasn't born yesterday, girl.' My mother's skeletal fingers grip my hands. 'You haven't done anything you'll regret, have you?'

'I promise I haven't. I just drank too much champagne,' I put my fingertips to my temples, 'and my head's pounding. I promise, I'll tell you everything tomorrow when I've had some sleep.'

The last time I remember lying to my mother was when I was nine and I had pretended I had brushed my teeth. Guilty and terrified of being discovered I had raced up the stairs to wet my toothbrush.

My mother's hands move up my arm urgently. She touches the tips of her fingers on the dark bruises on my arm, while her worried eyes burn into mine. 'Where did these come from?'

'That's not him,' I explain nervously.

'The road to hell is paved with good intentions,' she warns darkly.

'I promise, I'll tell you everything tomorrow, but it's not what you think.' Really it is worse, a little voice says. 'All will be well, you wait and see,' I say brightly and smile.

My mother does not return my smile. Instead she gazes at me sadly.

'Goodnight, Mum. I really love you.'

'I love you too.'

I stumble down the short corridor to my room, and making it to the edge of my bed, drop the shoes clutched in my hands. Then, like a tree that has been felled I fall onto the top of my bed and am almost instantly inside a deep, dreamless sleep.

Six

The muted but insistent ringing of my mobile phone jars me awake. For a moment I lay crumpled and confused on my bed. My head is banging furiously. Then I pat the duvet around me, locate my purse and pulling my phone out squint at the number. It is the agency.

I sit up, clear my throat, and say, 'Yes?'

'Hello, Lana. It's Jane here.'

'Hi, Jane.'

'Well, we've received a disturbing and very serious accusation from your current employer. They have also requested a replacement to finish the booking. So please do not go into work today. Mrs. Lipman would also like to see you to sort out this situation. Can you come in later today?'

I remember Blake telling me to keep the day free. 'Not today but tomorrow.'

'Oh.' There is a surprised pause. 'All right. What about ten thirty tomorrow?'

'OK, see you then.'

I gently ease my head back on my pillow. Listening carefully I hear my mother moving around the flat, and sigh. I will have to go out soon and face my mother and tell fresh new lies, but I feel so tired I fall back to sleep.

Again it is the phone that wakes me. I lift it up to my face. It is a number I do not recognize.

'Hello,' I croak.

'Miss Bloom?' a woman's voice enquires. Her voice is extremely efficient and professional. And wide awake.

'Yes.'

'Laura Arnold, Mr. Barrington's personal assistant, here. Is this a good time for you to talk?'

'Yes. Yes, of course.' I jerk upright and take a gulp of water from a bottle by my bedside.

'Mr. Barrington has asked me to make some appointments for you today. May I run through them with you now?'

'What kind of appointments?'

'Tom Edwards, Mr. Barrington's driver, will be around your flat at ten forty-five. Your first stop will be your doctor where you have an appointment to see the nurse.'

'How do you know who my doctor is?'

There is a pause. It is pregnant with possibilities, perhaps even explanations.

'It doesn't matter,' I say quickly.

As if she has not been interrupted, the woman continues, 'She will discuss various contraceptive options with you if you are not already on some form of birth control. Next, you have a meeting with Mr. Barrington's lawyer. Once you have concluded your business there, you will be dropped off at our publicist, Fleur Jan's office. Ms. Jan will take you shopping and then on to your appointment with the hairdresser. After that Tom has instructions to take you to a beauty salon where you are booked for a full body wax, manicure and pedicure. Please bear in mind that Mr. Barrington does not like garish colors. He prefers light colors, but likes French manicures best.

'When you are done at the salon, Tom will take you to the apartment in St John's Wood and show you around. Please do settle in. The fridge and cupboards will be fully stocked, but should you require, I can also arrange for a meal of your choice to be delivered to you from one of the local restaurants. It would be advisable to eat lightly as Mr. Barrington gets into London late evening, and he wishes to take you out for supper about nine p.m. He tends to be very punctual so do be ready by eight thirty. Do you have any particular dietary needs or preferences?'

'No.'

'Food allergies?'

'No.'

'Good. Would you like me to order your dinner?'

'No, I'll make do.'

'Fine. Do you have a passport?'

'No.'

'You will need one.'

'Why?'

'Mr. Barrington travels often and I believe you will be required to accompany him on some of those trips.'

'Uh… I see.'

'I will make the necessary arrangements for you and contact you tomorrow.'

'Thank you.'

'Oh, and when you go to meet the solicitor please take some form of identification with you. Do you have any questions?'

'Er… No. I don't think so.'

'If you do come up with any question or requests call me on this number. I will be happy to assist.'

'OK. Thanks, Miss Arnold.'

'It's Mrs. Arnold, actually. Have a nice day, Miss Bloom.'

I let myself fall backwards and feel a surge of wild surge of joy inside me. I begin to grin. He has not changed his mind. It seems almost impossible to imagine but I have pulled it off. Raised the money.

Mother *will* go to America.

Still, I never expected such competence or thoroughness. This is more like a business takeover than the simple transaction I had envisaged. Naively, I had thought up the oldest scheme in the book, imagining visits to seedy hotels or an odd-smelling flat somewhere in London, probably Soho, but with brutal efficiency he was drawing up my reality to mirror his unemotional world where everything is black and white, and every effort must be made to stop any sort of gray in the form of confusion or disorder creeping in.

I glance at my alarm clock. I must have been more tired than I had realized. It is already nine thirty even though it is another gray day outside. I hold my tender head in my hands. A couple more paracetamols should do the trick.

I sit up, swallow them down and lying back on the bed close my eyes and remember last night. The details are fuzzy. Only the kiss remains crystal clear. I remember his eyes—how unaffected he was. If not for that pulse drumming madly in his throat I would have thought he had felt nothing. Eventually, I can no longer put off meeting my mother so I drag myself out of bed and pad to our shared bathroom. The tiles are sickly green and one or two are cracked, but everything is sparkling clean.

The orange dress is badly crumpled. I take it off and carefully hand wash it in the sink. After wringing it out, I hang it inside the bath, and get in it myself. I turn on the shower head, and hold the warm stream over my body.

When I come out, I feel like a new person. Quickly, I slip into clean underwear and dress in jeans and a white shirt. Then I comb my hair, tie it into a ponytail high on my head and with a last look in the mirror I brave the kitchen.

'Morning, Mum. How are you feeling today?' My voice is bright.

My mother smiles at me. 'Today is a good day.'

I smile back. Both of us look forward to the good days. The good days are what keep us going.

'Didn't you have to go to work today?'

'Nope. Got fired yesterday.'

My mother shoots me a surprised, worried glance. 'Sit down. I want a word with you.'

I sit and she puts a bowl in front of me. 'Is this man really giving us the money?'

'Unless he backs out,' I say and pour some cereal into the bowl.

'What's his name?'

'Blake,' I reply pouring milk.

My mother sighs. 'Are you purposely making this hard?'

'All right. His name is Blake Barrington.' Casually I sprinkle two spoons of sugar on my cereal.

'Barrington?' My mother's forehead creases into a frown. 'Why is that name familiar?'

I finish chewing before I answer. 'Because it's that famous banking family,' I mumble, and quickly spoon more cereal into my mouth.

My mother gasps and sits on the chair opposite me. There is something in her eyes I have never seen before. 'How long have you been seeing him?'

'I met him yesterday.' More cereal gets immediately shoved into my mouth. I want to end this conversation as soon as possible.

'You met him yesterday and he agreed to give you fifty thousand pounds.'

'Mmnnn.' I make a production of munching.

'Why?'

'Guess it must have been love at first sight.'

My mother's eyes narrow dangerously. 'Is there something you are not telling me, young lady?'

'Nope. The rest are all gory details,' I dismiss cheerfully.

But mother is not put off. She is like a hound that has scented blood. 'How old is he?'

'I didn't ask, but he didn't look a day over thirty.'

'So he's not an old man?'

'Definitely not.'

'When do I get to meet him?'

I slip out of my chair with my empty bowl and go to the sink. 'Soon, Mum. Very soon,' I say, quickly rinsing the bowl and spoon.

My mother sits at the table as still as a statue. 'Does Jack know?'

'Jack?' I turn to face her. 'We're not boyfriend and girlfriend, you know.'

'I know, I know but…'

'But what?'

'Well, I always assumed you'd end up with him.'

'We don't feel that way about each other.'

She sighed. 'You just seem so right for each other. I always dreamed that he'd be my son-in-law.'

'Since when?'

'You could do a lot worse than him, Lana. He's tall and handsome and he'll be a doctor soon.'

'I'm not marrying Jack, Mum. He's like my brother.'

'The path of true love is not always smooth,' she insists stubbornly.

I go into my bedroom, put the orange coat on a hanger, pick up the orange shoes off the floor, and go out of the front door, saying, 'Popping over to Bill's.'

Seven

The door next to our home is open and I enter it without knocking or calling out. The air is full of the smell of bacon cooking. A big woman wearing a faded apron in the kitchen shouts out to me.

'Morning, Jane,' I greet and take the blue stairs two at a time. Billie has been my best friend since we were in primary school, and I have been taking these stairs all my life. I don't knock on Billie's bedroom door, but enter and shut it behind me.

Billie's room has exactly the same view and dimensions as mine but it has been done up in myriad colors and is perpetually messy. When it is clean, it reminds me of a piece of modern art. I hang the orange coat on a hook behind the door, open a cupboard, put the shoes inside and close it. Then, I carefully sidestep over a mess of clothes and a pizza takeaway box to sit at the edge of the single bed.

Billie has her head buried under a pillow. She was born nondescript with pale eyes and mousy brown hair and given the equally nondescript name Jane, but when she was eleven years old she reinvented herself. She turned up in school one day, her hair bleached white and turned into an Afro.

'Why have you done *that* to your hair?' the bad, white boys taunted.

'Because I *like* it,' she said so coolly and with such confidence that their opinion no longer mattered. She became a law unto herself and changed her name to Billie knowing that it would be shortened to Bill. Then she found a tattooist in Kilburn High Street, who agreed to tattoo a spider on her left shoulder.

'Wouldn't a butterfly have been better? Spiders are so creepy,' her mother worried. But more and more spiders crawled onto her back, down her thin left arm, and eventually a few small but intrepid ones began to climb up her neck. Now Bill Black has given up the Afro, but her hair is still dead white and her lips perpetually crimson.

'Wake up, Bill,' I say.

Billie mutters something. It sounds very much like fuck off, but I know to be persistent.

'I've got something to tell you,' I say, and shake her shoulder firmly.

'What time is it?'

'Nearly ten.'

Billie extracts her crown of white hair from under the pillow. 'This better be good,' she grumbles and hangs her head off the side of the bed with her eyes still shut.

'Come on, Bill. I've only got thirty minutes.'

'Pass me a fag,' she mumbles, and makes a silent snarl with her lips. I take a cigarette out of a box I find by the bedside, light it and put it into the curve of her snarl. She inhales lustily.

I stay silent until Billie has sat up, propped up some pillows behind her, and is leaning back against them. 'OK,' she says, 'did you do it?'

I nod.

Billie's eyes pop open. 'Whoa.... You did....? And you got the money?'

I grin.

Billie almost chokes on her cigarette. 'I don't believe it! The fat bastard agreed to cough up fifty grand?'

'Actually, it wasn't him.'

Billie holds a palm up. 'Back up, back up. What?'

'OK, I did ask him, but he turned out to be a total perv; you won't believe what his idea of a good time is. Fortunately, someone else cut in and offered double what I had asked him.'

'Bloody hell!' screams Billie.

'Keep your voice down,' I whisper. 'Your mother's in the kitchen.'

'Double, as in a hundred thousand pounds?'

I nod a lot.

'So who is this guy then?'

'Have you heard of the Barringtons?'

'Who?'

I walk to the laptop sitting on Billie's messy desk and, flip it open. When the familiar Google emblem pops up on the screen I type in Blake Barrington. As the page starts to load I carry the laptop over and hold it out to Billie. Billie grinds out her cigarette in an overflowing ashtray and takes it wordlessly.

She whistles low and long and looks up at me with shining eyes. 'Oh! Mr. Bombastic, call me fantastic. I thought all the best-looking males were gay?'

I blush. 'Pick the Wikipedia entry,' I advise.

Billie hits the Wikipedia link and proceeds to read aloud from the screen.

'The Barrington banking dynasty, also referred to as the House of Barrington is one of the world's oldest existing banking dynasties with a history spanning over four hundred years. The family is descended from Lord John James Barrington.

'Unlike the courtiers of earlier centuries, who financed and managed European noble houses, but often lost their wealth through violence or expropriation, the new international bank created by the Barringtons was impervious to local attacks.

'Their strategy for success was to keep control of their banks in family hands through carefully arranged marriages to first or second cousins. Similar to royal intermarriages, it allowed them to maintain full secrecy about the size of their fortunes. By the late nineteenth century, however, almost all of the Barringtons had started to marry outside the family into other great, old families.

'The family is renowned for its vast art collections, palaces, wine properties, yacht racing, luxury hotels, grand houses, as well as for its philanthropy. By the end of the century, the family was unparalleled in wealth and luxury even by the richest royal families.

'The Barringtons are elusive. There is no book about them that is both revealing and accurate. Libraries of nonsense have been written about them. An author who planned to write a book entitled *Lies About The Barringtons* abandoned it, saying, "It was relatively easy to spot the lies, but proved impossible to find the truth."

Billie pauses and lets her eyes skim down the screen. 'Well, the rest seems to be stuff about their international investment banking activities, the mergers they have been involved in, and is as interesting as a man in a wet T-shirt. Yup, and more shite here about them being one of the oldest institutions operating in the London Money Market.'

Billie yawns hugely.

'It just goes on and on about their…hedging services…worldwide assets… Boring, boring… Holding companies…Swiss registered. Boring, boring, primarily a financial entity but…largest shareholders in the DeBeers…a virtual monopoly of quick silver mines. Ah! Here is something a little more meaty. In 2008 the group had one hundred billion in assets! God! Can you imagine having that kind of money? No wonder the great, great grandson is spending it like water.

'Oh look. Some pictures. Wow! Get an eyeful of how the rich live.'

She turns the laptop around so I can look at the images as she scrolls down.

'Just some of their chateaus, palaces, castles, garden-mansions and city houses. Wow! Look at this one in St James' Park.'

There is silence for a while as we gaze in wonder at the photos.

'Do you think you will get to visit any of these places?'

'Definitely not. I have to sign a confidentiality agreement.'

'Still, it's an unbelievably exciting prospect, isn't it? Just don't fall for him.'

'I won't,' I say confidently.

'Let's skip back to Google and go to about…page three…and see what the conspiracy theories have to say about this august family. Oh dear…blood-sucking crew.

"If my sons did not want war, there would be none." His grandmother said that. Very nice."

Billie shuts the laptop. 'OK, quite enough of this. Let's not spoil a good thing. Let's celebrate your total brilliance, instead.'

I open my mouth to protest. I know exactly what Billie means by celebrate.

'Aaa-aaa… Don't say another word,' she says, reaching under the bed to pull out a bottle of vodka. She opens the drawer of her tiny bedside table and rummages around until she finds two dirty shot glasses. She puts the two glasses on her bedside table, which is marked with leftover circles from other vodka full glasses. These glasses will make new moons that overlap the other moons.

She fills them to the brim and holds one out to me.

I laugh. 'So early in the morning?'

'Are you kidding? This is an un-fucking-believable turnaround. You go out of here in borrowed plumes to snare a fat bastard and you come back with not just the most eligible bachelor on either side of the Atlantic, but the son of the richest family on earth. You've pulled off the deal of the century, girl. We have to celebrate,' she says firmly.

'I haven't pulled him, Bill. He wants to have sex with me in exchange for money.'

'So? Would you rather be having sex with the hunk or the perv?'

I say nothing.

'Look, I know you are into that deluded saving yourself for the special guy nonsense, but honestly, love, you really are getting too old to be playing virgin. Every puss needs a good pair of boots otherwise it shrivels up and dies.'

I smile. 'You don't have one.'

'Ah, but I have Mr. Rabbit. Nothing dies while he is around.' She opens the second drawer of her bedside cabinet to expose her huge and colorful dildo.

I gasp. 'With your mum in the next room?'

She shrugs. 'I use it when she's at the supermarket.'

I take the proffered glass, still shaking my head at her total lack of inhibitions. We clink glasses.

'Here's to…' Billie grins wickedly. 'Hot sex with anyone.'

We down the vodka and Billie thumps her chest. So early in the morning the alcohol has an immediate effect on me. Heat spreads quickly through my veins and makes me feel light-headed. The future seems exciting suddenly.

Billie's mother yells, 'Breakfast is ready,' from downstairs.

Billie lets her head hit the pillow behind her in disgust. 'God, she does my head in. If only she wouldn't do that. Every fucking morning she goes on about breakfast. You'd have thought after nineteen years she'd know I don't eat that shit.' She twists her body and reaches out to the little cupboard under the drawers of her bedside cabinet and takes out a jar of strawberry jam and a spoon. She unscrews the lid and feeds herself a spoonful of jam.

I open my mouth.

'Don't say it,' Billie warns.

'I won't, but really, Billie, your mum's right. How can you eat jam for breakfast?'

'For the one thousandth time because it's *delicious*.' She spoons another mouthful in, and commands, 'Now, tell me every inappropriate thing that happened last night. Don't leave a single thing out.'

I tell her everything except for the kiss, which I myself cannot quite make sense of yet and cannot bring myself to talk about. Billie's eyes alight on the orange coat and she smiles smugly. 'I told you the dress and coat were lucky. This is what you wanted, right?'

'Yeah, it's what I wanted. More than anything else in the world. You're still OK to travel with my mum, aren't you?'

'Of course. I love her too, you know.'

'Thanks, Bill.' My voice breaks.

'Don't thank me. I'm going on an all expenses paid trip to America! Yee…haa…'

'I don't know what I'd do without you and Jack.'

'Talking about Jack, what and when are you going to tell him?'

I sigh. 'Everything, this weekend.'

'He won't be happy.'

'I know, but he'll understand. I've got no choice, Bill.'

'I know, babe.'

'Bill, thanks again for agreeing to accompany my mum. I really don't know what I'd do without you.'

'There's a big, black car parked outside,' Jane hollers.

Billie leap-frogs to the end of her bed and, standing on her bed with her palms resting on the windowsill, cranes her neck to look out into the street below. 'Jesus, Lana, that's a Bentley with a driver in a peaked cap.'

I look at the clock face. 'That'll be my ride. Got to go. Call you later.'

Billie sits on the windowsill, exhales and, through the smoke says, 'Say hello to banker boy for me, won't you?'

I run down the stairs and find Jane standing at the bottom of them. Her round, red face looks quite animated. 'Is that car here for you?'

'Looks like it,' I say as I disappear into my own home. I pick up my rucksack, make sure my ID is in it, kiss mum goodbye, and run out towards the waiting Bentley.

Eight

The driver is standing outside the car by the time I get to it. He touches his cap. 'Miss Lana Bloom?'

I nod breathlessly.

'Good morning. Tom Edwards,' he says, by way of introduction and opens the back door for me. I sink into the fragrant, immaculately pale interior and he shuts the door after me. Along the building I see the heads of all my neighbors poking out of their windows.

I lean back. The leather under my palm is soft and cool. Tom gets into the front and looks at me in the rearview mirror. He has soft brown eyes that crinkle in the corners. He takes a white envelope from the passenger seat and twists around to hand it to me. 'Our first stop is the doctor. This is for him.'

'Thanks,' I say, taking the letter. It has my doctor's name written in blue ink and is unsealed. The glass that separates us closes and the engine hums into life. I open the letter and read it. It is a request for my medical records.

My mobile lights up.

'Hey,' says Jack. His voice is bright and full of life.

'Hey,' I reply matching his brightness.

'What's wrong?'

'Nothing. Why?'

'Come on… I know you better than that. Spit it out, Lana.'

'OK, but not on the phone. Are you coming down this weekend to see your mother?'

'Yeah.'

'Well, I'll tell you then.'

'No, you won't. I'll come by my mum's for dinner. You can tell me then.'

'I've got a date.'

There is a silence. 'Really? That's great. Anyone I know?'

'You don't know him, but you might have heard of him.'

'Well?'

'Blake Law Barrington.'

'*The* Blake Barrington?'

'Yeah.'

'You've got a date with a Barrington? How? What are you not telling me, Lana?' He sounds worried.

'It's not really a date, but I can't tell you on the phone.'

'You're not doing anything stupid, are you?' he asks apprehensively.

'No, Jack. I'm not. I'm doing the only thing I can do.'

'It's something to do with your mum, isn't it?'

'Yeah.'

'Oh! Shit, Lana. You didn't.'

'I did.'

'You're better than this.'

'Jack, my mum's dying. She's stage four. She doesn't have months to live. The doctors have given her weeks.'

'Oh, Lana. Can't we borrow the money?'

My laugh is bitter. 'Who can I ask, Jack? Jerry? And if I ask Jerry what will I need to do for the money?'

'What do you need to do for the money now?'

'What I am doing won't land me in prison. It's just sex, Jack.'

Jack goes silent.

'It won't be for long.'

'How long?'

'It's for a month.'

'That long?'

'It's a lot of money, Jack.'

'Don't give the shit a day more than a month.'

'I won't. I've got to go, but I will see you during the weekend. And thanks for caring about me.'

'It's just a bad habit.'

'Jack?'

'Yeah.'

'I miss you, you know.'

'Just be safe, Lana.'

'Bye, Jack.'

'Bye, Lana,' he says and there is so much sadness in his voice that I want to call him back and reassure him that it isn't so bad. I am not selling my soul, only my body.

In the doctor's surgery I pass over the envelope and am ushered into a room with the nurse who asks and performs the necessary blood tests with brisk efficiency. Afterwards, she discusses several options and recommends Microgynon.

'Take it from today. Since your last period ended two days ago you should be protected immediately, but just to be safe use a condom for the next seven days,' she advises. Twenty minutes after I entered that small blue and white room I have a prescription for three months' supply of contraceptive pills.

The receptionist has an envelope for me. It is addressed to Mr. Jay Benby. This letter is sealed.

I thank her and go outside. Tom jumps out of the car and opens the door for me before going around the back of the car and getting into the driver's seat.

'If you give me the prescription, I'll pick it up for you while you are at the solicitors.'

For some strange reason I feel the heat rush up my throat.

'I have daughters your age,' he says kindly, and I lean forward and hand him the prescription. 'Thanks, Mr. Edwards.'

'No worries. And call me Tom.'

'Er… How long have you been working for Mr. Barrington?'

'Going on seven years now.'

'Is he… Is he a fair man?'

Tom meets my eyes in the mirror. 'He's as straight as a die,' he says, and by his tone I realize that he will volunteer no more than that. I turn my head and watch the people on the street.

The solicitor's offices are in an old building in the West End. I am surprised to note that it is not the slick place I expected. The hushed air of importance, mingled with an impression that nothing much ever happens here, makes it feel more like a library. A receptionist shows me into Mr. Jay Benby's room.

The room smells faintly of air-freshener. The carpet is green, his table is an old antique inlaid with green leather, and the old-fashioned, mahogany bookshelves are filled with thick volumes of law books. Behind Mr. Benby there is a dark, rather grim painting of a countryside landscape in a gilded frame. The painting is so old that the sky is yellow in some parts and brown in others.

Mr. Benby rises from the depths of a deeply padded black leather chair. His grip is very firm and his smile serves as a polite welcome. He is wearing a dark, three-piece suit and a red, silk tie. And his hair—what little is left of it—has been carefully slicked back.

He waves his hand towards one of the chairs in front of his desk and I see that he is wearing a ring with a large, opaque, blue stone on his little finger. It strikes me as incongruous. I remember a story my mother once told me.

He was rich and wore a turquoise ring from Nishapur on his little finger.

Everything else about Mr. Benby and his office says, *Trust me. I'm good for it.* The opaque ring alone screams, *I'm a liar.*

After exchanging brief pleasantries he pushes a stapled, thin bunch of papers towards me. 'Here is your contract.'

I look at it. *Consensual Sexual Acts and Confidentiality Agreement.*

'You are within your rights to take it home, read it yourself and if you prefer, get your own lawyer to look at it, but no amendments can be made to it.'

I bite my lip and eye the contract. 'Can you show me where it says I will receive the hundred thousand pounds?'

He appears surprised. 'Of course.'

His kind obviously don't talk about money openly. They just bill you. He turns the contract to its second page and puts a clean, blunt finger to the clause that I was asking for. And I see that it clearly states that I will be paid the sum as soon as I sign the contract. I look up at Benby. 'Do you have a pen?'

His eyebrows rise. 'Don't you want to read it first?'

I shake my head.

He looks at me disapprovingly. 'This agreement has been drawn up so there is never any…misunderstanding. You must be fully aware of the gravity and nature of the contract you are about to sign and agree to abide by its conditions. There are some clauses in there that are of utmost importance.'

'Like what?'

'The most important being the confidentiality understanding. This clause means that you will never be able to write a book, sell your story, or reveal any personal details about Mr. Barrington or his family. There is no information, even outside of sexual activities, that may be revealed to anyone. Not even friends or family. You can never bring a guest to the apartment you will share with Mr. Barrington. This clause applies to family, friends and acquaintances. In the event that they reveal anything, you will be held liable.'

He stops and flips the pages of the contract.

'Please pay particular attention to this section,' he says stabbing a stubby finger on the paper. 'It expressly prohibits any form of recording device while in the company of Mr. Barrington.'

I nod.

He clears his throat. 'And you must practice some form of birth control. In the event that you get pregnant you must terminate the pregnancy immediately.'

I stare at him. What kind of people are these?

Undaunted by my astonished face the lawyer carries on talking, 'You must understand that this contract is binding. At the dissolution of your relationship you will not receive anything more than is already stipulated in this contract. Other than the agreed sum you will not seek further financial gain, notoriety or advancement in any form as the result of this relationship. Breach of contract or failure by yourself will result in immediate termination of the agreement, and in the case of breach, the offended party may seek all remedies available at law or in equity. This section shall survive termination of this agreement and remain in effect for the rest of your life.'

'Fine.'

'One more thing. Mr. Barrington wanted me to emphasize that the contract will be for three months.'

'I thought it was going to be for one month?'

The lawyer's face does not change. 'Your services will be required for the period of three months.'

I press my lips together. I was very drunk last night, but I am sure he said one month. 'Can I speak to him?'

'Of course.' He picks up the phone and speed dials his client's number. 'Mr. Barrington, Miss Bloom would like to have a word about the length of the contract.' He pauses to listen to something Blake says. 'Yes, she has.' Then he passes the phone to me and quietly leaves the room. I wait until he closes the door before I speak. I am dismayed to hear my voice sound uncertain and timid.

'Hello, Blake.'

'Hello, Lana.' His voice is different than I remembered. Colder: he seems a total stranger.

I swallow. 'About the duration of the contract. The lawyer says…' I begin.

'Sorry, Lana, but that is not negotiable,' he says, not sounding sorry at all.

'Oh.'

'Was there anything else you wanted?'

'Er… No.'

'Well, have a good day then, and I will see you tonight.'

There is a click and the line goes dead. I replace the phone slowly. It dawns on me then that Scott Fitzgerald was right—the rich are different. They are unashamed by their ruthlessness. The lawyer, who must have been watching an extension light, walks into the room.

'All sorted out?'

'Yes. Where do I sign?'

'You do realize that you will have to read it at some point as there are other clauses than the ones we have discussed in there that you must adhere to.'

'Yes.'

'Do you acknowledge that you have received, read and understood the terms and conditions outlined, and agree to abide by the said terms?'

'Yes.'

'All right,' he drawls and looks at me expectantly. And I realize he has opened the contract up at the last page.

'Sign here.'

I sign. My hands are dead steady.

'And date it here.'

I date it.

He opens another contract. 'Sign and date again, please.'

When I raise my head he is watching me steadily. He smiles coldly. It occurs to me that he believes his dealings with me to be beneath him. I am expensive trash. He has thoughts about me that are supremely unflattering.

'Well, that's that, then. Here is your copy.'

He presses a buzzer that brings his secretary. 'Helen here will take your bank details and tell you everything else you need to know.' He half stands and holds his hand out. 'Thank you, Miss Bloom. Please do not hesitate to call me if you have any further queries.'

In the back seat of the Bentley, I find a Boots bag and inside it my prescription. I ask Tom to stop at a cash machine. I pop my debit card into the hole in the wall and can hardly believe it. One hundred thousand and thirty-two pounds, seventy pence. By heaven!

Nine

'Hi, I'm Fleur Jan,' the publicist says, coming forward, her hand held out to me.

'Hi,' I greet with a smile.

Fleur's eyes are very large, a much deeper blue than mine, and are enhanced by false eyelashes that she bats with great effect. Her hair is cut very short around her lovely face. Dressed in a brown pencil skirt and a pink top she is effortlessly chic.

'What we will be doing today has nothing to do with publicity for the company, but Mr. Barrington knows how much I love shopping so he asked if I wouldn't mind going shopping with you. Of course I said yes,' she explains with a twinkle in her eyes.

'Cool,' I say, some of Fleur's enthusiasm already rubbing off on me. Fleur is a good change after the drawling Mr. Benby.

'Mr Barrington mentioned formal attire, beachwear and a pair of new trainers.'

I nod. Wow, he remembered the trainers. The man is thorough, I will give him that.

'Do you want a coffee or tea or shall we hit the road?'

'Hit the road.'

We walk together to the lift. Fleur calls it and turns to me. 'Do you have any specific shops or do you want to leave it to me?'

'You decide everything.'

And that turns out to be an excellent decision as Fleur proves to be an expert shopping companion. She knows exactly where to go to get what.

Our first stop is Selfridges. Fleur guides me towards a cosmetics counter.

'This girl is a genius. She can make a chimp look sexy, so listen carefully to her advice,' she says about a sweet-looking lady standing behind the counter called Aisha.

I am popped on a high stool, given a hand mirror and taught how to make the best of my make-up.

'Have you ever tried wearing waterproof mascara?' Fleur asks smoothly. Her face is innocent, but it is clear that Blake has mentioned something about my smudged mascara.

Together the three of us choose two lipsticks, some sparkly eyeliner, cream blusher and waterproof mascara.

'Now to the perfume department,' directs Fleur. 'Something terribly exotic to go with your dark hair and gorgeous eyes.'

Afterwards, Tom drops us off at the front entrance of Harrods. I have never been inside before, but Fleur seems to know her way around, and we quickly make for the first floor where we pick up what Fleur calls the basics: a white blouse and plain black trousers. We walk out of the side entrance of Harrods on the east side and enter Rigby and Peller. Fleur has made me an appointment for a fitting. The woman who calls me into the changing room is middle-aged with large strong hands.

'Most women are walking around in the wrong bra size,' she says, and makes me bend over while she fits me with a bra. It turns out so am I. I am not a 34A but a 32B. When I have chosen the designs I want Fleur flashes her company credit card.

'Now let's go get the good stuff,' she says, batting her eyelashes.

'How much are you allowed to spend on me?' I ask curiously.

'Actually,' she says, 'Mr. Barrington didn't see fit to set a limit.' She winks conspiratorially. 'So we make hay while the sun shines.'

We walk around the back of Harrods and down Old Brompton Road. Fleur is a mine of information. She knows everything about fashion, what's so in, what's so out, what's in if you are not really in, what gets the best second-hand prices when you want to flog it.

She suggests a beautiful red and silver handbag in Gucci. 'To die for,' she says.

'It is a limited edition. Pure crocodile skin,' explains the snooty-faced sales assistant helpfully.

'OK,' I agree, bewildered by the price tag. I stand by the counter while Fleur pays and wonder what sort of reception I would have received if I had come here alone.

'Let's go,' Fleur sings merrily.

Then I am being led into Chanel. All my life I have dreamed of owning a Chanel bag. Once someone gave me a fake Chanel bag for Christmas and I waited until a reasonable time had passed before giving it away to a charity shop. If I can't afford the real thing I don't want to pretend.

Fleur is clever. It is as if she understands; here her suggestions are unnecessary. All she says is, 'Choose.' I feel I am in Aladdin's cave. It is impossible to choose, but in the end I pick the classic black with the leather interlaced gold chain strap. When Fleur goes to the counter she says, 'And we'll have that pink one too.'

'That's nearly seven thousand pounds!'

'Yes, but we have no limit. Besides, every girl needs a pink handbag. What else can you carry when you want to dress in white?' Fleur argues reasonably. She phones Tom to come and pick up the packages.

Almost in a daze, I am led into and out of a string of designer boutiques. Most of the shop assistants seem to recognize and head for Fleur immediately.

'Cupboard love,' Fleur dismisses, as they flutter around her with accommodating smiles. 'I am often here helping the wives of our high profile Middle Eastern clients spend their money.'

Fleur seems very sure of exactly what will look good on me. We buy a cream and gold suit, a red cocktail dress; a backless, sequined, black evening gown, and a sleeveless signature dress from Pucci, and of course shoes to match. Fleur decides that I will need a black pair of court shoes for the trousers, dainty diamond-studded stilettos, two tone sandals, tall brown boots, and multi-colored, ultra fashionable platforms.

‘Right, we are almost running out of time, but first a quick trip to Versace. Versace can be too gaudy and whorish, but this season they have something that I think will suit you perfectly.’

That something turns out to be an electric blue silk shirt that is almost the same color as my eyes and skin-tight black leather trousers.

‘Exactly as I thought—fantastic,’ she says, pleased with herself. She looks at her wristwatch. ‘Perfect timing. Let’s have some tea.’

Once again Tom comes to collect the packages, and we find ourselves a table in a French patisserie full of women. We order cream tea. I bite into a buttered cream and jam filled scone ravenously.

‘It is wonderful that you can eat so much and still be so slim. I have to be careful,’ Fleur says, sipping lemon tea and breaking off small crumbs of her croissant.

‘Missed lunch,’ I say, swallowing.

Once I catch Fleur looking at me with an unreadable expression.

‘Do you have to do this often for Blake?’ I ask.

‘To be perfectly honest, I have never done this before or heard of Mr. Barrington asking anyone else to do something similar, and though I was flattered to be asked, I was also dreading it. I thought you would be a brash gold-digger, but you are an unassuming breath of fresh air. It has been a delight to take you around.’

After tea, Fleur and me climb into the Bentley and Tom takes us to a hairdressing salon that belongs to one of the top hairstylists in the country. We walk into the perfumed space and a young girl with bright red hair comes to greet and lead us into a private area. Two glasses of champagne arrive on a tray.

‘Go ahead,’ Fleur encourages. ‘You’ll be grateful for it when you are at your next appointment.’

‘Why? What’s next?’

Fleur smiles cheekily. 'Full body wax.'

My jaw drops when the celebrity stylist himself appears. He noisily air-kisses Fleur on both cheeks and does the same with me. Then he stands back to look at me thoughtfully. Tipping his head slightly to the side he reaches for my hair.

'Oh,' he exclaims, rubbing it between his fingers. 'Virgin hair. You have never bleached or permed it, have you?'

I shake my head.

'It is a sin to cut such hair. Come, come,' he says leading me to a single chair in front of a mirror and waiting while I sit. 'We will leave the length, but we will do something wonderful for this heart-shaped face. We will give it a fringe.'

He picks up his comb and scissors. When he is finished I can hardly believe what a difference a fringe has made. My eyes are suddenly enormous and my little chin now looks delicate and cat-like.

'Beautiful,' declares the stylist flamboyantly.

'Very beautiful, indeed,' agrees a smiling Fleur.

While Fleur is paying, I stare at myself in the mirror. It is truly amazing how much a fringe can change one's face. I look so different I almost don't recognize myself.

'This is where I say goodbye,' Fleur says from behind me. I turn around to face her. 'Tom will take you to the beauty salon where you have your last appointment. That over with, he will take you to the apartment where you will soak in a lovely bath and then you will dress in your new clothes. I believe you have a hot date at nine.'

'Thank you, Fleur.'

'The pleasure was all mine.'

'I don't know if we will ever meet again, but I'll never forget you.'

'Nor I you,' she says, and bending forward plants a light kiss on my cheek.

My next stop is in High Street Kensington. In an all-white salon an olive-skinned, middle-aged, barrel-like woman in a white trouser uniform with a clipboard, smiles and introduces herself as Rosa Rehon. Rosa is Spanish and has retained her thick accent despite having been in England for fifteen years. She shows me into a small room with a beautician's bed.

'Ever had a full body wax before?'

'No.'

'No problem. We use three different waxes here. For the longer hair, the medium length, and for the pesky short ones.'

The waxes are heating in three pots. Each one is a different color.

'Shall we do waist down first?'

'Will this hurt a lot?'

'Well, it depends on your pain threshold. Some people fall asleep while I am waxing them.'

'Really?'

Her pearly whites flash. 'Really. Pop on board. We will start with the legs.'

I reluctantly climb on the bed that has been lined with paper, and lie down.

Rosa paints a thin layer of warm wax on my calf and lays a strip of cloth on the wax. 'Ready?' she asks.

I nod and she rips.

'Ow,' I cry.

'The first one always hurts. The next one will be better,' she says.

She paints another layer of wax and, stretching my skin, rips it off.

'Ow,' I cry again.

'It gets better after a while,' she consoles unconvincingly, and launches into a monologue about how she and her husband have jam sandwiches every night while they are watching TV. 'Sometimes, on weekends we will turn to each other and say, "Shall we have another?" and we do,' she enlightens.

Despite a penchant for innocuous jam sandwiches, Rosa turns out to be a hair Nazi. She will not tolerate even the smallest hair anywhere. A painful hour later, I am red and hot and stinging all over. I have been asked to assume embarrassing positions so any stray hairs around what Rosa calls the bum hole can be ripped off.

'Why would anyone want to do that?' I ask.

'It looks prettier this way,' Rosa says, as she rips another offending hair out.

My reply is another cry of pain.

When it is all over Rosa squints at my face. 'I can do your eyebrows for free,' she offers. 'Eyebrows don't hurt at all.'

'Yes, I know. Some of your customers fall asleep.'

Again a flash of strong teeth. 'Well, shall I? I can make them look very beautiful.'

'OK.'

The Rehons have a son in art school apparently, and Rosa fills me in about him while she works on my eyebrows. When she is finished she applies aloe vera gel before bringing a round mirror and giving it to me. The skin looks red and a little swollen but Rosa is right—my eyebrows actually arch and frame my eyes rather fetchingly.

After that torture the manicure and pedicure are a pleasure. I watch the orange nail varnish that Billie so painstakingly painted onto my fingers and toes yesterday get wiped away. On the drive to the apartment I examine my French manicure and have to admit it is very pretty.

The car comes to a stop at a tall white building with a glass-fronted entrance.

'Here we are,' says Tom, switching off the engine.

Ten

The reception is plush with deep, cream carpets and chandeliers in every hallway. There is an Indian guard slumped behind a desk reading a newspaper in a foreign language who immediately straightens and stands to attention. Tom introduces me.

'Lana, this is Mr. Nair.'

Tom turns to Mr. Nair. 'This is Miss Bloom. She will be living in the penthouse for the next three months. Please ensure that she will be well taken care of.'

Mr. Nair smiles broadly. 'Certainly. That will be my number one priority,' he says in a strong Indian accent while shaking his head like one of those nodding dogs in the backs of people's cars. He turns to look at me. 'I am very pleased to meet you, Miss Bloom. Anything at all that you need, please do not hesitate to ask.'

We shake hands, then Tom accompanies me into the lift. He inserts a card key into a slot and hits the top floor button. I lean against the shiny cold brass handrail while the lift silently races upwards. When the lift doors whoosh open, he allows me to exit first, and then precedes me into the corridor. The corridor is thickly carpeted and tastefully wallpapered in beige and silver.

'There is only one other apartment on this floor,' Tom explains and opens the door. He deposits the shopping bags on the floor by the doorway. 'I will go and get the rest of your shopping and then I will show you how everything works.'

I close the door behind him and lean against it.

Wow! Just wow!

A long corridor with richly enameled walls seems to lead to a light-filled room. As if in slow motion I let my fingers trail on the cool, enameled surface as I walk down the deep white runner carpet towards the glorious light. With the evening sun pouring in, I stand at the doorway to what is the living room, and look at my surroundings in wonder. At the imposingly high ceilings, the amazing glass walls that lead to a wide balcony laid out with a table, chairs and potted topiary. At the mirrored wall that reflected the elegant silver patterned pale lilac wallpaper, the rich furnishings, and the deep-pile, white carpet.

It is so massive, so hugely extravagant and luxurious it is as if I have walked into a page of a glossy magazine. I turn when I hear the door opening.

Tom puts the rest of my shopping on the floor and walks towards me. 'Beautiful, isn't it?'

'Yes, very.'

He takes me around the spacious four-bedroom apartment and shows me how everything works. Which buttons on the remote cause the curtains to open and close and which one makes a gorgeous painting rise onto the wall to expose a TV screen. There are buttons for the shutters, buttons for working the wine cooler, buttons for the lights, the media room, and for the coffee machine. I nod and make sounds to indicate I have understood, but it hardly registers. The opulence overkill has numbed me.

'Any problems, just call the caretaker. The number is over there,' he says finally, indicating a card that has been placed on a side table near the front door.

'Thank you.'

'Be back for you at eight thirty. Mr. Barrington hates people to be late.'

'Don't worry, Tom, you won't have to hang around waiting for me. I'll be ready.'

I close the door, find my mobile, hit home, and wait for my mother's soft voice to answer.

'Hi, Mum,' I say brightly.

'Where are you?'

'I'm at Blake's apartment.'

'Oh! When are you coming home?'

I swallow. This will be the first time I will not return to my own bed. I know it will be difficult for my mother. 'Not tonight, Mum. I won't be home tonight, but I'll be there first thing in the morning.'

First she goes silent. Then she expels a soft sigh. 'All right, Lana. I will see you tomorrow. Be safe, daughter of mine.'

'See you tomorrow, mum.'

I walk down the enameled corridor and go into the main bedroom. It is very large with a huge bed. The décor is deep blue and silver. I kick off my shoes and walk barefoot on the luxurious carpet towards the bathroom. The bathroom is a green marble and gold fittings affair. There is a Jacuzzi bath and a large shower cubicle. By the washbasin, lush toiletries still in their packages, have been laid out for my use. I unwrap a pale green oval of soap and wash my hands.

Afterwards, I open cabinets and find them all empty. I go back into the bedroom and walk through to the walnut dressing rooms. The built-in wardrobes are all as bare as the bathroom cabinets.

So he does not live here.

This is a place purely for sex.

I walk out of the bedroom and head for the kitchen. It has been done up in sunny yellow with glossy black granite worktops and surfaces. There is an island in the middle and stools around it. When I was young I dreamed of such a kitchen. I perch on one of the tall stools, swivel around a few times, and hop off. I venture to a cupboard and open it. It is full of stuff—expensive stuff that is never found in my poor mother's cupboards. Tins of biscuits from Fortnum and Masons, Jellies from Harrods, French chocolates with fancy names. I take a few down and admire the exquisite packaging.

Then I shut the cupboard and turn towards the fridge. More exotic stuff: truffles, hand-made blue cheeses, gooseberries, cuts of dried meats, wild smoked salmon, a dressed lobster, caviar… The vegetable drawer is packed with organic produce. Even the eggs have blue shells. There are two bottles of champagne lying on their sides. I take one out and look at the label. Dom Perignon.

'Hmnnn…' I say into the silence.

Carefully, I peel back the foil and the wire that holds down the cork. Holding the bottle between my thighs I twist the cork as I have seen the waiter do, but it takes many tries, and when it finally pops out, I have shaken the bottle so much, it sprays everywhere.

I clean up with some paper napkins, and finding a glass in one of the cabinets pour myself a drink. Carrying the glass I go back into the living room, slide back the doors, and step outside. I stand there for a long while looking at the wonderful view of the park and surrounding area, but I can feel no joy in my heart. My thoughts are with my mother. Eventually I close my eyes and pray that all will be well.

I raise my glass to the sky. 'Oh, Mum,' I whisper, 'be well again.' Then I bring the glass to my lips and drink to my mother's health.

There is not enough time to try the Jacuzzi bathtub, so I have a shower. The showerhead is wonderfully powerful unlike the weak one I am used to. The shower invigorates me and I go through my shopping bags with some measure of excitement. The bruises from the night before mean that I am only able to wear the Versace silk shirt. I pull on the tight leather trousers that end at my ankles and slip on the strappy stilettos.

Then I do my eyes the way Aisha taught me to and paint my lips soft pink. I am so nervous my hands tremble slightly. Dressed, I go back into the living room and pour myself another glass of champagne.

At eight thirty sharp the bell rings.

Tom comes in with a large, flat cardboard box, which he carefully places on the side table. 'I was asked to drop this off for Mr. Barrington. You look beautiful, Miss Bloom,' he compliments awkwardly.

'Thank you, but will you call me Lana, Tom?' The champagne has made me feel light-headed and I smile at him mistily.

'Of course, Lana,' he says smiling.

The reception desk is no longer manned by Mr. Nair. A small, white man with beady, suspicious eyes is introduced as Mr. Burrows. He smiles politely, but distantly. This was a man who did not want to get involved with any of the occupants of the building.

After that Tom drives me to a private club in Sloane Square called Madame Yula.

Eleven

Blake cuts a dashing if remote figure at the bar. He is wearing an oyster gray lounge suit and a black shirt, and is even more disturbingly attractive than I remember. He stands when he sees me and I stop, frozen by his eyes. Neither of us moves. It is as if we are again in a world of our own. Just his smoldering eyes and my strong desire for more from him—what exactly I do not quite know. Then he breaks the spell by moving towards me.

'You look edible,' he purrs, his eyes lingering on the curve of my hips.

I blush and touch my bangs.

'I like the hair, too,' he murmurs.

'Thanks.' My voice sounds nervous and shaky.

He reaches a hand out to touch me and instinctively I pull away. I had not meant to, but my body has its own reactions to him.

He drops his hand and eyes me coldly. 'Look,' he says. 'We can make it a totally sex thing or we can dress it up a little and it will look pretty in the corner. It's up to you. It's all the same to me.'

Pretty in the corner. Strange turn of phrase. I study him from beneath my eyelashes. 'Dress it up a little,' I say.

'Good. Can I get you something to drink? A glass of champagne? You're partial to it, if I remember correctly,' he says, and leads me to the bar.

I look around the bar. It is decorated in dark wood and deep red curtains. It actually looks like an old-fashioned French brothel. 'I've already had two glasses.'

His eyebrows rise. 'You found the alcohol.'

'It found me. I opened the fridge and there it was begging me to drink it.'

His eyes twinkle. 'Yes, alcohol has a habit of doing that.'

'I'm hungry, though.'

'Let's get some food into you then.'

We are shown into a private booth. The sommelier arrives and I listen to Blake order a bottle of wine that I have never heard of, and realize that the poor and the middle classes have been conned into believing that Chablis, Chateauneuf-du-Pape, Pouilly Fume, and Sancerre are superior wines for the discerning, but the truly rich are imbibing a totally different class of drink.

He picks up the menu and my eyes are drawn to his wrists. They are so utterly masculine they make my stomach tighten.

'How was your day?' he asks.

'I don't want to sound ungrateful, because I really am *very* grateful, but why did you buy me so much stuff?'

He leans back in his chair. 'Did you have a doll when you were young?'

'Yes.'

'Did you make little clothes for her?'

'Yes.'

'Did it give you pleasure?'

'Yes.'

'Why?'

'I don't know. It was my doll and I wanted it to look good.'

'That is how I feel about you. You are my doll. I like the idea of dressing you the way I see fit. I want you to look good. Besides, I like that every stitch on your body has been paid for by me.'

I feel a frisson of electricity run up my spine. 'I'm not a doll.'

'To me you are. A living, breathing doll.'

'What happens in three months' time?'

'Did you eventually get bored with your doll and stop playing with her?'

'Yes.' My voice is soft. I know where this conversation is going.

'So will I and when I do I will put you aside as you did your doll.'

'Well, that's clear enough.'

'Good.' His face is expressionless. 'What would you like to eat?'

I look at the menu. There is fish and chicken. I hope he will order one of those. But there is also foie gras, which I'd rather die than eat. The waiter appears at Blake's side. 'Are you ready to order, monsieur?'

Blake looks at me enquiringly.

'I'm just going to have whatever you're having,' I say breezily.

'Mussels in white wine to start followed by the herb crusted lamb cutlets.'

'Pommes sables or pommes soufflé?' the waiter enquires.

I look blankly at Blake.

'Try the potato soufflé,' he says. 'You might like it.'

'OK, potato soufflé,' I agree. When the waiter is gone, I take a sip of wine. It must have been good, but I am so nervous I register it only as a cold liquid. 'So,' I begin, 'You are a banker.'

'And you have been on Google.'

'Wikipedia actually. I was curious. All my life I imagined bankers were thieves utilizing fractional reserve banking to create money out of nothing, and then they take your house and car and business when you can't keep up the repayments.'

'Ah, this is like all bankers are thieves, all lawyers are liars, and all women are whores.'

'I'd rather be a whore than a banker.'

'That's handy then. I'd rather be a banker who buys a whore.'

'Why do you need to buy a woman, anyway? With that flashy car of yours, they must be leaving their phone number by the droves on your windscreen wipers.'

'You were an impulse buy.' His eyes crinkle at the corners. I amuse him.

I look at his perfectly cut suit, his beautifully manicured hands, and the Swiss precision watch glinting on his wrist. 'There is nothing impulsive about you.' My eyes take in that delectable lock of hair that falls over his forehead. 'Other than your hair.'

He laughs out loud. I look at him. The man has lovely teeth.

'This might turn out to be a lot more interesting than I thought,' he says.

The mussels arrive in tiny, covered black pots. When Blake opens his I follow suit. The smell is maddeningly good, but I wait until Blake reaches for his utensils before I copy him.

'Bon appétit,' he says.

'Bon appétit,' I repeat.

The mussels are meltingly soft in my mouth.

'Good?' asks Blake.

'Very.'

But the portion is so small it is quickly gone. 'I don't understand something,' I say, daintily dabbing the corners of my mouth. 'How come the paparazzi never follow you around like they do other celebrities and eligible bachelors to expose all your escapades and wrongdoings?'

'For the same reason my family and the other great families are not on the Forbes richest list. We don't like publicity. Unless it is sanctified by us you won't see it in the papers.'

'Are you trying to tell me your family has that much power?'

'I'm not trying to, I'm telling you. It's easy when you control the media.'

'Your family controls the media?'

'The great, old families do. It is in our interest to work as a group.' His eyes glitter in the soft light.

Suddenly his lips twitch. He leans back and flashes a smile. 'But enough about me. Tell me about yourself.'

'What do you want to know?'

'Other than the fact that you live on a council estate and don't earn enough, I know nothing at all about you.'

'That's not strictly true. You know I am AIDS free, don't have any sexually transmitted diseases, own a clean bill of health, am on contraceptives as of today, and have had a full body wax.'

His smile becomes a wolfish grin. 'How was the waxing session? Not too painful, I hope.'

'Not at all. You should try it sometime.'

He laughs outright. 'The day you pay me to have sex with you, I will.'

I don't smile back.

The lamb arrives. I look at my plate. Blood has eddied under the meat. I cannot eat that. I sigh inwardly. It will be vegetables and potato again.

'Where do you get your unusual coloring from?'

'My grandmother on my mother's side was Iranian. The hair is from her and the blue eyes are from my father's side of the family.'

He lets his eyes wander around my face, lingering on my mouth. 'Have you been to Iran before?'

'I went once as a child, but it is my dream to take my mother back there.'

'It's dangerous there now.'

'For you maybe, but not for me or Mum it isn't.'

'Still, don't you think you should wait until all this talk of war is over?'

'There will be war. It is better to go now, before Iran becomes another Iraq or Libya.'

'What was it like when you were there?'

'When I went it was a wonderful place. We stayed in the desert. It was very beautiful. At night there was pure silence. And the sand dunes sing.'

'You can go to Saudi Arabia for sand dunes.'

'You don't understand. Isfahan is in our blood. I remember when my mother was leaving she climbed to the top of the steps of the plane, then she turned around and did this.' I open my arms out as if to gather something in the air and bring my arms back towards my face and kiss the tips of my fingers. 'I asked her what she was doing and she said she was kissing the air of her motherland goodbye. I remember thinking even then that I must bring her back to that beloved land of hers.'

'I've never been to Iran.'

'Of course you haven't. Iran doesn't have a central bank. My mother says it is why the world wants to wage war with it.'

'Does she also believe Elvis is still alive?'

My eyes flash and I glare at him. 'We can dress this arrangement up and play it any way you want to, but don't you dare criticize my mother. Even the dirt at the bottom of her shoes is better than you,' I cry passionately.

He gazes at my flushed cheeks and glittering eyes without anger, almost speculatively. 'You brought her up,' he says softly.

My anger subsides as suddenly as it came. 'Yes, I did,' I agree flatly, and must have looked as lost and as naïve as I felt for he reaches out to cover my hand with his. I pull mine away.

He takes his hand back to his end of the table and looks at me coldly. 'OK, have it your way,' he says, and looks for the waiter.

A waiter appears almost immediately.

The waiter looks at my plate. 'Was everything all right, mademoiselle?'

'It was fine. Just not hungry.'

'Perhaps you have left some space for dessert?' he suggests with a tilted head.

I shake my head and the waiter looks at Blake. 'Monsieur?'

'Just the check.'

'Of course,' the waiter says with a nod, and raises his eyebrow to another waiter hovering by a pillar. The man comes and begins clearing away the plates. The bill is presented discreetly in a black wallet and Blake drops his card into it. When his card comes back, Blake says, 'Shall we?'

He stands and, with his hand on the small of my back, leads me out.

Twelve

The drive is completed in tense silence. When we get into the softly lit apartment, Blake tosses his card key on the side table and turns to me. 'Money's in the bank?'

I nod.

'We're good?'

I nod again.

'I gave you what you need; now you will give me what I need.'

I nod, ashamed by my own rudeness. It was a deal and he did keep his side of it.

'I'll pour us a drink. Change into those and meet me in the bedroom,' Blake says, gesturing towards the flat box that Tom brought in and put on the side table earlier. Then he turns his back on me and walks down that beautiful corridor into the living room.

I take the box and turning into the first door in the corridor, make my way into the main bedroom. Someone has come in and turned on the bedside lights, and turned down the bed. I go into the bathroom and close the door. Inside the box are wisps of lace and silk. I take them out.

A little dress in some transparent white material, an all lace bra, a thong, suspenders and silk stockings and a pair of platform shoes very similar to the ones I was wearing the night we met. Except for the fine baby blue ribbons on the suspenders, everything is in pure white. I glance at the size on the bra.

Of course. 32B.

I slip out of my clothes and get into the bra and suspenders. Then I carefully pull on the stockings. I have never worn suspenders before and the little hooks are fiddly and take me a long time. I hear a noise in the bedroom. Blake has already come in. Nervously, I pull on the lacey white knickers and look at myself in the mirror. I can hardly believe it is me. I rinse with mouthwash, take a deep breath and, opening the door go into the bedroom.

And just stand there staring, my heart crashing against my ribcage.

Good God! He is lying shirtless on the bed, propped against pillows, all sexy and toned and… and bristling with animal magnetism. There is not an ounce of fat on that sleek body. This is definitely not a man who imbibes Hobnobs. His legs are crossed at his ankles and his eyes are hooded. There is no expression in his face and no way of knowing what he is thinking. There is also something very bad and exciting about being in that lush bedroom with a cold, cold banker who has paid for you.

'Come closer,' he invites.

Clubland chart music is playing in the background. 'Give Me a Reason' by Pink and Nate Ruess comes on. Pink is singing, *Right from the start you were a thief. You stole my heart. And I your willing victim.*

I walk slowly into the middle of the room: my stomach is in knots: my mouth is dry: my eyes are saucers.

When I am two feet away from the bed, he says, 'Stop.'

I stop.

'Strip. Slowly.'

I freeze with shock.

He laughs. The sound is soft but carries some hint of cruelty. He is the cat playing with a mouse. From his position of dominance and control he says, 'I won't say relax, I'm not going to eat you, because I am.'

I straighten my back and step out of my platforms.

'No,' he commands. 'Not the shoes. Keep those on.'

Silently I step back into them. I can hear the blood pounding in my ears. No man has seen me nude. I untie the ribbon in front of the diaphanous dress and shrug. It slips off me, whispering and sighing.

For a moment I stand in my lacy underwear, suspenders and stockings.

Pink and Nate are belting out, *Just give me a reason. Just a little bit's enough.*

For a second I think of Billie saying every puss needs a good pair of boots, and I tell myself, sure, why not? It is just sex. I twist my hands behind my back and take my bra off. Let it dangle at the tip of one finger before I let it drop.

I see his chest rise with an indrawn breath, and I slip the fingers of both hands into the bit of lace and string and ease it slowly down my legs. I come up slowly resisting the urge to cover myself with my hands.

'You have a very, very beautiful body, Lana Bloom,' the man on the bed says. His voice is thick with lust.

We're not broken, just bent. And we can learn to love again.

I face his gaze again. His eyes are eating me alive. I have never seen hunger like that.

'Turn around.'

I turn around.

You're pouring a drink. No, nothing is as bad as it seems.

'Now spread your legs.'

We'll come clean. We're not broken, just bent.

I step outwards.

'More.'

I oblige. My calf muscles strain to hold the position in the high shoes.

'Bend forward.'

I bend.

'Touch the floor.'

I spread my fingers, lay them on the floor, and hear his gasp. For some long seconds I am bent forward, my legs spread far apart, and my ass high in the air. His eyes are a hot tingle on my exposed skin. The pose is blatantly demeaning. I should feel degraded and humiliated. Instead there is an unfamiliar heat between my legs. And my belly is clenched with feral excitement.

'Come here.'

I drop to my knees and crouching low, turn around. He is sitting on the edge of the bed. I stand and go to him. His strong hands span my waist and before I know it I am travelling in the air. I land on the bed with a slight bounce and a shocked gasp. On my back I watch him with widened eyes. His eyes are black and impenetrable. His body hard and big, the muscles rippling.

'I own you,' he says possessively. 'You're mine to do with as I please.' Then he pins me on the bed and I watch with even wider eyes as he takes off his trousers and steps out of his boxers, a truly magnificent creature.

I stare at his cock with fascination. It is thicker than my wrist and huge. Will it fit inside me? He picks up a condom by the bedside, tears it open, and puts it on. Then he bends over me, opens my legs and stares at my opened, freshly waxed pussy. I feel my body tremble with anticipation.

'What a beauty you are.' He runs his fingers along the slit of flesh. It opens out further. 'Like the petals of a pink flower,' he purrs.

I flush with excitement.

'Soaking wet.' He takes his fingers out and puts them in his mouth. 'And as I expected: sweet.'

My heart is hammering in my chest.

'You want this too,' he says so softly I have to strain to hear him. 'As much as me.' And I realize that he is right: I do. I want him as much as he wants me. I want from him what I have never wanted from any other man. I want him inside me, stretching me, possessing me.

I stare transfixed at his angrily throbbing, erect dick. I want all of that inside me. My hands come up and touch it. Rock hard but silky.

That small and tentative response from me drives him over the edge. 'Sorry,' he grates suddenly. 'I just can't do foreplay this time.'

He put his hands on either side of me and plunges into me. The shock of his sudden entry makes me cry out in pain. He hurt me. A lot.

He freezes. The ferocious lust is wiped away from his eyes. 'Fuck,' he swears, and pulls out of me.

I cannot help it. Tears well up in my eyes and escape down the sides of my temples. Ashamed to the core, I close my eyes.

'Why didn't you tell me?'

'You didn't ask,' I sniff, feeling incredibly stupid.

His hard length shifts and he sits facing away from me. 'It will be better next time,' he says, and without touching me or attempting to comfort me, stands and begins to dress. Rejected and defeated, I watch his strong V-shaped back, the beautifully proportioned buttocks, and the columns of his muscular legs as he shrugs into his shirt. He buttons it as he walks to the door.

He cannot wait to get away from me.

It is obvious that I am a great disappointment to him. I should have asked Billie for some lessons on how to pleasure a man. Instead I have lain there like a pillow and then worse still, I screamed when he entered me. I cover my cheeks with my hands. Oh, the shame of it. And this was what I saved up for. A fine mistress I was going to make. I hear the door close and I am all alone in that stupendous apartment.

Blake Law Barrington

I punch the button on the elevator and curse audibly. I am in a state of shock. It is unbelievable, but I never suspected that air of untouched innocence was not cultivated. I pull my hand down my cheek to my chin. I should never have been so rough. I treated her like a common prostitute.

Strange how badly I want to go back into that darkened bedroom and to kiss that trembling mouth. How much I want to wipe away those tears, take her in my arms and hold her until she falls asleep. But a larger part of me hates the way I feel. The sick pull she has on me irritates and angers me.

It is unnatural. I have been with hundreds of women, some as beautiful, and others sexually accomplished, but none of them have done this to me. I don't want to *feel* for her. I am glad I have left her body. Away from her essence I can think rationally.

Still I shouldn't have done what I did.

I got carried away and lost myself in what seems to be a growing and undeniable need to possess her completely. I don't exactly understand why, but whenever I am near her, I lose all my carefully cultivated 'cool'. All I want to do is drag her by the hair to my bed and fuck her until she is so sore she is screaming for me to stop. What I want is to have total control of her body. And why shouldn't I? I have paid for the privilege. The urge is strong now, I tell myself, but it will lessen with every single coupling.

She will never be more than a three-month itch.

A bottle-blonde is walking down the corridor towards the lift. The occupant of the other penthouse is an Arab sheik. I glance at her. She is wearing a tube top and white leggings. Her boobs are obviously fake, but she is beautiful in a hard sort of way. The way a mistress should be.

I think of Lana again. The way the helpless tears escaped. I had not expected that. I can't understand it. Why would a virgin be propositioning someone like Lothian for money? For the first time I wonder why she had wanted the money.

The lift arrives and I stand back to allow the woman to enter first. She has a good arse. She turns around in the lift and our eyes touch. We neither smile, but her mouth twists. The air becomes thick with her unspoken invitation.

I let my eyes travel down her body and convince myself Lana is not special. Even this one will do too. Nothing has changed.

I will marry Victoria. I take my phone out of my pocket and leave a text for my secretary:

Red roses—Lana.

White roses—Victoria.

Thirteen

Lana Bloom

'I'm baking a cake,' my mother says.

'You are?' There is a brightness in my voice. My mother only bakes when she is feeling good.

'Lemon, your favorite.'

'Oh good.'

'What time are you coming home?'

'I'm leaving now, actually.'

'Good. I want you to take a quarter over to Jack's mum.'

'OK. See you in twenty minutes,' I say and after putting a jar of blackberry jam, two tins of biscuits, and a box of fancy chocolates into my bag, leave the apartment. I take the bus to Kilburn.

As I am running up the steps I meet Jerry's sister who calls out, 'Heard you snagged yourself a rich boyfriend.'

'Not quite,' I reply, and before I can be bullied into a confessional conversation step aside, saying, 'Sorry, Ann, but got to rush.' I run past her taking the shallow steps two at a time. Already the curtain twitchers have spread the story.

I turn my key in our blue door and am greeted by the fragrant smell of my mother's baking. It is instantly familiar and dear. This is my home. My mother is at the kitchen sink washing dishes.

'Hey, I can do that for you.'

'No, I'm finished,' she says, turning the tap shut and snapping off her rubber gloves. She faces me, but her eyes, assessing, careful, and worried, change when she sees me.

'Oh my God!' she cries. 'Your hair. I can't believe how beautiful you look.'

I smile at her. 'I missed you yesterday.'

'Have you had breakfast?'

'Yeah. I brought some stuff for you.' I reach into my knapsack, bring out the tins of biscuits and chocolates and put them on my mother's small kitchen table.

My mother comes forward, but she does not touch the food. Instead she looks at me. 'Did you steal this?' Her voice is no more than a whisper.

'Mum!' I cry, shocked. 'What are you saying? Blake's secretary bought all this for me and I brought some back for you.'

She sinks weakly into a chair. 'Sorry. Sorry, Lana. Of course, you would never steal. I've just been so worried about you. Everything is so different. I don't know what to think anymore.'

The oven pings and she stands, but I push her down gently.

'I'll get it,' I say, and donning the oven gloves, take the cake out. It smells divine and is nicely risen. I close the oven door, put the cake on the metal rack and lean against the sink. 'Shall I put the kettle on? We need to talk.'

Mum nods and I set about making the tea. While the tea is boiling I lay cups and saucers. Everyone else in the estate drinks from mugs except my mother, who always uses a cup and saucer. I pour the boiling water into the teapot and carry it to the table. When the tea has brewed I pour it out into two cups. Then I open a tin of biscuits from Fortnum and Masons and hold it out to my mum. My mother's thin, pale fingers hesitantly take one. She bites into it and chews.

'Nice?' I ask.

My mother nods slowly.

'You're going to America on Wednesday, Mum.'

My mother puts the biscuit down beside the saucer. She links her hands tightly on the table and faces me. 'I'm going nowhere until I know exactly what is going on. Exactly how you are getting all this money? And what you are doing for it?'

'I explained last night. The man I am seeing has given it to us.'

'Who is this man who has fifty thousand pounds to spare?'

'Mum, he's a millionaire many times over. He gave me double what I asked.'

She stares at me aghast. 'You asked him for money? I didn't bring you up to ask strange men for money.'

'Yeah, I asked him and so what? I didn't force him or steal it.'

'Well, I don't want it. I'd rather shrivel up and die than use this dirty money.'

I stare at my mother in shock. Her face is set in the stubborn lines that I know mean that her mind is made up. It cannot be changed. I swallow the lump in my throat and stand suddenly. 'You'd make me an orphan for your stupid pride,' I accuse.

My mother blinks suddenly, the wind taken out of her sails.

'Are you going to sit there and tell me that if I was dying and had a few weeks left to live you wouldn't have asked a filthy rich stranger for a bit of money?'

My mother says nothing.

'High and mighty ideals and principles are all right when you are not utterly, utterly desperate, Mum.'

'You didn't just ask him, did you? Tell the truth. You prostituted yourself.'

'Assuming that I did. And I didn't.' I say a little prayer for my lie. 'Wouldn't you have done the same for me?'

My mother begins to cry softly. 'You don't understand. You will, one day, when you have your own child. I am not important.' She beats her chest with both her hands. 'This is just worm food. I won't have you sully yourself for this destroyed body. You are young. You have your whole life ahead of you and I am going to die, anyway.'

'No, you're not,' I whisper fiercely.

'But I am. And it's time you accepted that.'

'Remember when Daddy left and I swore to take care of you?'

My mother's eyes become bleak. 'Yes.'

'Would you have me break my promise?'

'I'm going for another bout of chemo on Monday.'

'What for, Mum? What for? That stuff is so dangerous it'll probably kill you before the cancer does.'

Her lips move wordlessly. Then she covers her mouth with one hand. 'Sit down, Lana,' she whispers. 'Please.'

I shake my head. 'No, I won't. What's the point? In all the time I was trying to find a way to keep you alive I never thought that it would be you that would stand in my way.'

I turn away from her and begin to walk out of the house. I have sold myself for nothing. I reach the front door and I hear my mother shout from the kitchen, 'Do you like him?'

I turn around and she is standing there, so frail and breakable my heart hurts. Now I can be truthful. 'Yes.'

'I'll go.'

I walk towards her.

'I'm sorry,' she sobs.

I take her poor wasted body in my arms and the tears begin to flow. Neither of us say anything. Finally, when I can speak, I choke out. 'I love you, Mum. With all my heart. Please don't leave me. You're my mum. I'd do anything, anything for you.'

'I know, I know,' my mother soothes softly.

'Oh shit,' I say.

'What?'

I step away from my mother, put my hand into my pocket and bring out bits of blue shell. 'I brought you a blue egg.'

My mother tries, she really tries hard, but a giggle breaks through. For a few moments I can only stare at the rare spectacle of my mother stifling laughter. Then I too crack up.

'Take that jacket off and go wash your hand,' my mother finally says. 'I'll make us a fresh pot of tea and we'll have some of those nice biscuits you brought.'

'They *are* nice, aren't they?' I agree, slipping my soiled jacket off and walking towards the sink.

I am wiping my hands on a tea towel when my mother says, 'And you'll have to bring that nice man—Blake Barrington, did you say—over to dinner.'

'Uh, yeah… When you get back from your treatment.'

My mother stops and looks at me. 'I'm going to meet that young man before I get on the plane and I'll have no more said on the matter,' she says firmly.

While we are having our tea I tell her about the appointment I have made for a wig fitting in Selfridges.

Unconsciously she puts her right hand up to her scarf. 'Oh,' she says. 'Will that be very expensive?'

I grin. 'We're not paying for it.'

And my mother laughs. For the first time in many months, my mother throws back her head and laughs. 'That's good. That's very good,' and while she is laughing she begins to cry. When I go to hold her, she takes a deep, steadying breath and says, 'I know what you have done for me. You have used your body as a begging bowl.'

For a moment I am struck dumb by my mother's perceptiveness. Then my great, great love for her intervenes and I lie and lie and lie. 'You only say that because you have not met Blake yet. He is beautiful and strong and kind. It was love at first sight. When I told him about you, he gave double what he knew I needed.'

My mother sighs. 'I pray to God that I will be alive for your wedding.'

I feel the hollowness spread through my body. It doesn't matter, I tell myself fiercely. So what if my mother will be disappointed? All that counts is she will be cured. I will forget this one in time and marry someone else, another who will not consider me so lowly that I am only fit to be hidden away like a dirty little secret. Someone with a beautiful heart like Jack.

Yes, someone like Jack.

Fourteen

I leave my mother's house and going past Billie's door run two floors down to ring Jack's mother's doorbell. While I am waiting for her to open the door I look down the railing, and see Fat Mary browning herself into an uneven shade of lobster.

Fat Mary is a big woman who lives in the corner downstairs flat and sunbathes topless in her garden, even though it is overlooked, by all the other flats in the block. Every Friday night she makes her hair big, stuffs herself into a tight dress and high heels, and goes to the Irish nightclub on Kilburn high street to find herself a bloke to bring home. Like clockwork they slip out of her door, all sheepish before lunch on Saturday.

All the little boys on bicycles always call out, 'Hey, Mary, how's your mary?' Her fat face never alters as she shows them her middle finger.

Jack's mother's face appears at the kitchen window. 'Oh, hello, dear,' she says with a smile, before she comes to open the door. She has the same beautiful eyes fringed by thick sooty lashes as Jack.

'Hi, Fiona. Mum sent you some cake.'

'How lovely. How is she feeling today?'

'It's a good day today.'

'That's good. Would you like to come in, dear?'

'Nah, I've got to run.'

'Well, you run along, then.'

'See you later,' I say and turning begin to walk away.

'Lana?'

I turn around. 'Yeah?'

Fiona hesitates and I hitch my bag higher up my shoulder and take two steps towards her. 'What's the matter?'

'I…um…heard…you…ah…found yourself…a… boyfriend. A rich boyfriend,' she says anxiously.

I shift from one foot to the other. 'I just met him, Fiona. I wouldn't call him a boyfriend just yet. It might not work out.'

Fiona's timid face falls. It is obvious she has been hoping that the rumor going around is not true. Her voice is very tiny. 'You will be careful, won't you, my dear? I wouldn't say anything normally, but you've always been such an innocent thing. And I thought to myself, even if I come across as an interfering, old busybody, I've got to say something.'

She takes a deep breath. 'You know, I've always said you are the most beautiful girl on this estate, if not in all of Kilburn, and you should have become a model, but rich men are greedy. One is never ever enough for them.'

I put my rucksack on the concrete floor and leaning forward hug the woman. 'Thank you for caring, Fiona. I don't know how I would have coped all these years if not for Jack, Billie and you.'

Fiona hugs me tightly. 'Oh, child, you are like my own daughter to me. What you did for Jack; I've never thanked you.'

I untangle myself from Fiona. 'What I did for Jack? It is I who should thank Jack. He's taken care of me and fought my battles since the day I arrived.'

'He will never talk about it, but the year you arrived was the year his father died, and he became quite unmanageable and surly. He'd taken up with a gang who stole, carried knives and drank alcohol across the railroads. I was afraid for him, afraid that he would turn out like all the other boys on the estate—jobless drunks and drug addicts. But then your family moved in and suddenly he changed. He took over the job of being your older brother, and suddenly I got my caring, beautiful son back and thanks to you he's going to escape this terrible estate and become a doctor.' Tears filled her lovely eyes.

'If I was useful to him then I am glad, because I don't know what my life would have been like without him.'

Fiona smiles proudly at the thought of her good son.

'I've got to go, but I'll be around tomorrow with a box of biscuits like you've never tasted before.'

'Oooo.'

I laugh. 'More like oo la la… They're French.'

'Goodbye, dear girl.'

I wave, and run up the stairs. My phone rings and I stop to answer it. It is Mrs. Arnold calling to say she has booked an eight thirty table for Blake and me at The Fat Duck. She reminds me to be ready by 7.30p.m.

'Thanks,' I say. I end the call and think, 'I've been reduced to another appointment in his diary.'

Halfway up the second flight of stairs I hear Kensington Parish call out to me. I pop my head over the side railing and see that he is standing at his bedroom window at almost eye level to me.

'What's up, Kensington?'

'Hey, Lana,' he says. 'Do you think your man will let me have a ride in that car of his?'

'Unlikely,' I reply and carry on running up the stairs even though I hear him shout pleadingly, 'Oh! Come on, Lana. You haven't even asked. It's a 0-77. It's custom made, Lana. Come on… Lana?'

Billie's door is open and her mother is outside watering her hanging baskets.

'She's in her bedroom,' she says, by way of greeting.

'Thanks,' I reply, and run up the worn blue carpet. I knock once and enter. Billie is using up a can of hairspray on her hair. The room is choking with the stuff.

'Jesus, how can you bear to breathe this stuff?'

'Open the window if it bothers you.'

I open the window and take a deep breath before facing the synthetic smell in the room. Thankfully, Billie has finished. Her white hair has now been sprayed into a stiff man's pompadour that will survive a hurricane. She looks at her reflection with satisfaction. Then she turns away from the mirror, switches off her small telly, and goes to sit on the bed. She pats the space next to her.

I sit next to her and put my bag down.

'Well, spit it out then. What was it like?'

'It was awful.'

'What? Sex with the loaded hunk was awful?'

'Can we talk about it in a minute? I need to talk to you about some important stuff first.'

'No problems.'

'You are still OK to travel to the States with my mum, aren't you?'

'Of course. Are you kidding me? I'd never get another chance like this. All paid.'

'Good. I'll sort the tickets out so you travel out on Wednesday. And Mum has an entire day to recover before her appointment on Friday. You don't have to babysit her the whole time. Go out sightseeing and do the touristy thing. You'll have to accompany her to the doctor, though.'

'Cool.'

'Oh! Before I forget. I brought something for you.' I dig into my bag and fetch the jar of blackberry jam.

Billie takes it from me. 'Posh jam? Wow, I've never had anything like this before.' She reaches over, opens a drawer and gets a spoon. She twists open the lid and dips her spoon into it. 'Wow, you get to have awful sex and I get to go to America and eat jam from Harrods. Brilliant. How long is your contract for, again?'

'Three months.'

'Are you sure you can't increase it?'

'Billie, don't be such a witch.'

She spoons more jam. 'Can we talk about your awful sex now?'

'He left as soon as he found out that I had never been with anyone.' I shake my head with the shameful memory. 'I was pathetic, Bill. I lay there like a lemon.'

'How do you mean? Didn't you have sex?'

'Sort of. As soon as he entered I sort of screamed in shock. It was so sudden and…well, painful, and he pulled out double quick.'

'What?'

I bite my lip. 'He just stopped and left.'

'What do you mean left?'

'He got dressed and left.'

'And said nothing?'

'He said, "It'll be better next time."'

'Fuck me. He didn't finish?'

'No,' I say uncertainly. 'Is that very bad?'

'Bad! He sounds totally fucked up. Nobody stops halfway for no good reason.' She chews her cheek and leans forward eagerly. 'Tell me what happened before he did the deed.'

I squirm. 'Well, he had me dress up in a white frock with white underwear and white stockings.'

'Oh. My. God,' Billie hoots and begins to cackle madly. 'He wanted a whore that he could pretend was a virgin, but when he found he had the real thing in his bed he freaked out and ran away. That is so funny.'

'It's not, actually.'

Billie sobers with impressive speed. 'Sorry, yeah it's not.'

'Bill, will you teach me some techniques?'

'I don't know what I can teach you. I don't do cock, remember?'

Then she looks at my distraught face and grins. 'OK, let's start with foreplay. Foreplay waist up has to be pretty similar, right?'

'OK,' I agree.

'The ear is wickedly horny. All kinds of things can happen when it is given a bit of attention. Run your finger along the rim like this.' She runs her finger along the rim of her own ear. 'Sometimes you can lick your finger first and afterwards gently blow on the wet rim. But the best effect can be achieved if you nibble your way gently all the way down to the lobe and then suddenly stick your tongue into his ear. If done properly that should drive him crazy.'

'Really?' I say doubtfully.

'You should practice on someone else. I'd let you practice on me, but I might start to really fancy you and that would be too weird.'

'Are you serious?'

'When you brush your teeth in the mornings do you ever look at yourself in the mirror? You're fucking stunning, Lana. If I met you in a club, yeah, I'd jump your bones. How about trying it out on Jack?'

'No, Jack is pissed off with me. He doesn't say it, but he thinks what I've done is no better than what a prostitute does.'

Billie looks sideways at me. 'I admire you for what you have done.'

'Oh well, he doesn't.'

'He's just mad because he's always had this older brother, dead protective complex about you. But the truth is we are all prostitutes. Some women will put out for an expensive dinner, another for a ring on her finger, or a better lifestyle. You did it to save your mother. That's a whole lot better than the rest of us, I'd say.'

'Thanks, Bill.'

'Oh, there is another thing you can do to banker boy. You can tie him up! You'd need a metal bed or a four-poster, of course. This bed here would be useless. I once tied Leticia to her bed and it was real good. I told her to strip naked then I blindfolded her and trussed her to the four corners of the bed. And while she was lying there full of anticipation, I calmly told her I was going out to the shops to get some chocolate, and that I was going to leave her bedroom door open. God, you should have seen the way she begged and then swore at me.'

She chuckles gleefully. 'Her mother had said she would be back in twenty minutes, you see. I stuffed her knickers in her mouth and went out. Made sure to close the front door with a bang too.'

My mouth drops open. 'That was some chance you took. What if her mother had come back and found her tied spread-eagled and naked on her bed?'

'Nah, I had met her mother going up the lift and she told me to tell Leticia that she was going to the hairdresser after the shops and would be at least an hour.'

'Was Leticia mad at you?'

'Mad at me. She was quivering like a school dinner pudding. I stuck the Yorkie bar up her fanny and ate it off her. She said it was the best orgasm she's ever had.'

I laugh. 'Oh, Billie. Somehow I don't think he's going to let me tie him to a bed.'

'You can still try the blindfold. It increases the sensation when you can't see. You could suggest a game. Put the egg timer on and he who climaxes first loses. When it's his turn, blindfold him and give him the best sucking he's ever had.'

'OK, maybe, I'll try that.'

'Let me know how it goes, won't you?' Billie says with a smile.

I look at my watch. 'I've got to pop into the employment agency so they can tear a strip off me for inappropriately offering myself to one of their clients, but before I go; you know the extra money Blake gave me? I've decided I want you to have half.'

Billie's eyes widen. It takes a moment for her to find her voice again. 'I'll take the free trip and I'll take the jam, but I'm not taking the money.'

'Remember when we were kids and we used to say if we won the lottery we'd share the money. Well… Isn't this like winning the lottery?'

Billie smiles at me. 'This isn't the lottery. Besides, what would I do with money?'

'You could go get your boobs done.'

'Very tempting, but…'

'No buts. Do you want me to turn into one of those people who are generous only when they don't believe they will ever have the money? Would you give me half if our positions were reversed?'

Billie thinks and grimaces. 'To be honest I don't know what I'd do. I think I'm just like everyone else, I want to go out, get wasted out of my mind and have fun, but you've always been different. You used to save up to buy violets when you were a child and take the bus to see paintings in the National Gallery. That was probably why I was drawn to you then, even though you wore boring clothes and read the book instead of waiting for the movie version.'

'While you painted the toenails of your gerbil bright red…'

'Hamster,' Billie corrects, and laughs.

'Whatever. I know you're on the dole and can't show that you have too much in the way of savings so I've opened an account in my name at the Abbey and here's the card. Use it as if it is yours.'

Fifteen

I am fastening my hoop earrings when I hear someone at the front door. Stomach churning, I stand away from the dressing table and look at my reflection. I am wearing my Pucci dress. The colors look good with my hair and I know I have never looked so fine, but my heart is in my mouth. I am so nervous my hands are clammy. I wipe them and rub lotion into them. Then I slip into my beautiful new Jimmy Choos and leave the bedroom.

I turn into the paneled corridor and hear him in the sitting room. He is looking down on the lighted view of London and has not heard my footfalls on the soft carpets. It is only when my reflection shows in the glass that he turns.

The crease of his pants leg looks very sharp and his shoes are beautifully polished. My eyes move upwards. He is wearing a navy suit and an open soft blue shirt. My gaze travels to his brown, strong throat towards the deliciously straight mouth and up to his eyes; dark and hooded and so full of secrets. They are watching me intently. My breath catches. The flowers he sent are behind him.

'Thank you for the flowers. They are beautiful.'

'Come here,' he says and half sits on the table behind him. His voice is very soft. There is something in it I do not understand. I am nineteen and he is a man of the world. I go willingly to him. He catches me by my waist and pulls me to him until I am trapped between his thighs. I feel the heat that comes off his body.

'I'm sorry,' he says. 'I didn't know.'

I shake my head, embarrassed. 'You weren't to know. It's my fault. I should have warned you.'

'You look very beautiful tonight.'

I blush like an idiot.

He watches me blush, making me blush even more, then runs his finger along my lower lip. 'Are you for real?' he whispers.

I look at him without comprehension. He wants to tell me something. But what? I don't understand him at all. We are worlds apart. Maybe I shouldn't try to understand. This will all end in three months.

Without warning the expression in his eyes changes. His mouth twists. Something cold creeps into his eyes. 'We'd better go or we'll be late.'

Feeling the change I step away from him. Now I truly do not understand. Hot and cold. Perhaps it is a game. But he will not beat me. I can survive three months. I think of my mother and say. 'Yes, we don't want to be late.'

He offers me the crook of his arm. His voice comes out hostile and clipped. 'Shall we?'

I bite my lip. Now he is inexplicably angry with me. Nothing makes sense. Why is he angry with me? Confused, I thread my arm through his and we leave the apartment.

The Fat Duck is nestled in the middle of the English countryside, in a place called Bray. The women are all dressed to kill and the men are in dark suits. I have never been anywhere so glamorous, but it is bitter sweet: I have lied to my mother. I am with this man as his whore. And all of this will come to an end in three months' time. A young man with a French accent settles us into a waiting area and offers us delicate little bites of food and two glasses of champagne. Waiters nod and greet Blake by name as they pass. Apparently he is well known in this establishment.

'They are called amuse-bouches, mouth amusements,' Blake explains and watches as I nibble on the tiny offerings of mushroom and hazelnuts with basil oil and salmon mousse.

'Well?'

'I don't think I've ever tasted anything so delicious in all my life.'

The sommelier comes to help select the wine that will perfectly complement the food we intend to have, but Blake knows exactly what he wants.

'The 1996 Clos du Mesnil.'

The sommelier seems pleased with Blake's choice. The wine is brought and presented to Blake. When he nods, it is uncorked and a small amount is poured into a deep glass and given to Blake. He swirls it, sniffs it delicately, and pronounces it acceptable.

A fifth of my glass is filled. I raise it to my lips and taste it. What passed for wine until now seem like abrasive mixtures of grape juice and vinegar. With complicated scents that delicately tease and a distinctively smooth taste that slides down my throat, the wine is truly splendid.

I study the menu with fascination. It is no wonder that this restaurant is so famous. It has a uniquely original menu. There is even something called the mad hatter's tea party with mock turtle soup, a pocket watch and a toasted sandwich. Then there is snail porridge, crab biscuits and quail jelly, chicken served with vanilla mayonnaise, shaved fennel and red cabbage gazpacho with mustard ice cream, and something else I can't recognize served with oak moss and truffle oil.

Blake chooses roasted foie gras to start. I sigh inwardly. I am not eating force-fed goose liver.

The waiter looks at me. 'I won't bother with a starter, thank you.'

Blake orders the lamb with cucumber.

'I'll have the same,' I murmur.

The waiter moves away, and Blake looks at me strangely. His eyes are pitying. 'You can't read, can you?'

My head tilts back. 'Of course I can. I am a qualified secretary.'

'What was I supposed to think? Jay told me you signed the contract without reading it and this is the second time you've ordered the same as me and you hardly touched your food the last time. Why?'

I decide to be honest. 'I don't know which utensil to use to eat what.'

He is so surprised, he leans back in his seat, and regards me quietly. Not taking his eyes off me, he raises a hand slightly. Immediately, a waiter comes to his side. 'The lady would like to see the menu again, please. And hold the earlier order.'

'Of course, sir.'

Blake carries on watching me until the waiter returns with the menu.

'Would you like a moment with it?' he asks.

'No,' I say. 'I know what I want. I'd like the mock turtle soup to start and the poached salmon.'

When he is gone, Blake says, 'With utensils always start with the ones that are furthest out from the plate and work your way in. I will help you.'

'Thank you.'

'So what have you done today?'

'Well, I got taken off the books for er…inappropriate behavior so I went off in search of another temporary agency.'

He frowns. 'I don't want you to work for the duration of our contract.'

'Why?'

'Because I want you to be available to me day and night. I might want to have you at three in the morning or between meetings in the afternoon,' he explains brutally, and I feel the most surprising sexual thrill clench at my lower belly. I want to be available to this man day and night!

'It should be no problem for you.'

'What's that supposed to mean?'

'Don't you live on an estate where nobody works and everybody just scrounges off the state?'

I shake my head in wonder. 'Wow, that's one sweeping generalization you've just made there!'

'Why, is it not true?'

'While I was a child growing up my teachers and the governmental offices where my mother had to go for her weekly handouts, in subtle and unsubtle ways, tried to force into me the opinion you have just expressed. That we were parasites.'

I look him in the eye.

'But I always knew there was something inherently wrong about any train of thinking that could so conveniently dismiss all the unemployed and dependent population as parasites. And yet we did seem to be living off others. Then one day I learned the true nature of the parasite and it changed my life.'

He raises an eyebrow. Arrogant sod!

I smile. It does not reach my eyes. 'I learned that a successful parasite is one that is not recognized by its host, one that can make its host work for it without appearing as a burden. As such it must be the ruling class in every capitalist society that is the real parasite.'

'How is my kind a parasite to yours?' he scoffs.

I take a sip of the wonderful wine that he has paid for. 'How much tax did your family pay last year?'

He leans back and regards me without flinching. 'We paid what was legally due.'

Now it is my turn to scoff. 'Let me guess. Almost nothing.'

He shrugs. 'There is nothing wrong with legitimate tax avoidance schemes. I don't see how we are being parasitical, because we won't let the government take what is hard won and rightfully ours, and pass it onto the bone lazy masses who don't want to work and expect others to fund their lifestyles. In fact, I'll go so far as to say the system in this country is mad. Girls have babies when they are teenagers so the government will set them up in a flat and pay them a stipend for the rest of their lives. Crazy.'

I shake my head slowly. 'Do you really believe what you are saying?'

'Of course. Do you think teenage girls getting pregnant to secure a home for life is right?'

Our food arrives. It looks more like a work of art than food. I reach for the rounded spoon that has been placed furthest away and Blake nods.

He picks up his knife and fork. 'I'm kind of waiting for your reply.'

'No, I don't, but we are not talking about badly educated teenagers from troubled homes who think that getting pregnant is the best way out of grinding poverty for them. The teenage pregnancies are a result of a system that has marginalized and refused a good education to the poorest sections of society. They are not parasites. They are desperate people who have been trained to think that that is the best they can get out of life. But your lot….'

'We actually keep the country going, creating jobs—'

'Sure, in China and other Third World countries. Slave labor jobs. Besides, you're a banker. You don't create anything.'

He shifts in his chair. 'Hang on, let me get this right; my family is parasitical for not paying astronomical taxes, and your lot are not parasites even though you don't work a day in your lives and live entirely on government handouts.'

'Have you ever thought that people can be poor by design. When a child is born on the estate, he is already doomed to repeat his father's life. He will bear that same angry, helpless attitude of his father and never amount to much. In school he will be taught only to be a good worker. And if he has even a bone of rebellion in him he will refuse and become a scrounger. My mother was educated in a different country and she was from the middle class so she taught me middle class values. Work, earn money, pay your own way.'

'So why do you work only part-time?'

'I do that because my mother is often sick and I am her primary carer.'

'What's wrong with your mother?'

'Cancer.'

'Oh.'

'She *will* make it,' I say forcefully.

He nods slowly. 'Are you a Muslim?'

I sit back and watch Blake while our plates are cleared away. The hard planes of his face have been softened. There is a mad desire in me to reach out and stroke his face. 'No, my mother is a devout Christian. I am an agnostic. So far no God has impressed me as benign and truly interested in the welfare of humans.'

'Main course,' announces the waiter, and plates are lowered onto the table.

My salmon is encased in a tiny square parcel made of liquorice gel, and looks almost too beautiful to eat. I lift the fish knife and cut it open. Inside, the fish is perfectly cooked. I slip a tiny morsel pass my lips, and am surprised by how delicate and silky it is on my tongue.

'I have a very big favor to ask you.' I say.

He raises his eyebrows.

'It is very important to me.'

'Sure,' he says.

'You agreed without knowing what I am going to ask?'

'When people say I need a very big favor it's bound to be a small thing. It is when they ask for a small favor that I start worrying. So, what is it you want?'

'My mother has invited you around to dinner. It's just the once. You will have to pretend to be my boyfriend,' I say so quickly the words almost run into each other.

'What sort of thing will I have to do to convince her that I am your boyfriend?'

'Just the usual. Hold hands, a quick kiss. Nothing too heavy.'

He smiles cynically. 'I think I can manage that.'

'Thank you. I owe you one. Maybe one day you will need a favor and I can do something to help you.'

'I'll remember that,' he says, and falls silent. But the silence is not uncomfortable and we finish our main meal without further conversation.

He orders the macerated strawberries for dessert.

'I'll have the same,' I tell the waiter.

Blake grins. 'I thought you might go for the Like A Kid In A Sweetshop,' he says.

'I nearly did,' I admit. 'Do you know what's in it?'

'Just a selection, I guess. Want to change your mind?'

'No.'

The dessert is so delicious I wish my mother could try it. After the handmade chocolates, the bill arrives. I catch a glimpse of it. It is over four and a half thousand pounds. That is more than my mother spends on food for a whole year. It must be good to be so rich. I look at Blake in shock. He raises his eyes and returns my look. His eyes are sultry and slumberous.

And suddenly he seems devastatingly, impossibly handsome, but so aloof and unreachable that it is almost as if I have my nose pressed against a glass window and I am looking in at something I can never have.

Just like the poor match girl from Hans Christian Andersen's fairy tale who had to keep lighting her last matchsticks to see the fantastically beautiful sight in front of her.

When the matches run out she dies.

Sixteen

He opens the door of the apartment and waits for me to enter. I walk in and stand with my back to him, waiting. I hear the thick click of the door, then he is standing behind me. His breath is on my neck.

'Mmmm… You smell so good,' he whispers.

I lean my head back and find his chest. Rock solid it is.

I hear the sound of the zip and my dress is pooling around my shoes. He unhooks my bra and frees my breasts. In a smooth movement he has scooped me into his arms and is carrying me down the long corridor. There is something so caveman and primal about being carried to be ravished that I have to bury my head in his wide chest so he will not see how unbearably excited and flushed I am. I have been claimed. Now I will be taken and possessed.

He kicks open the bedroom door and lays me down on the bed.

Then he brings his mouth down on mine and kisses me ferociously. The feel and heat of his mouth is a shock to my system. Every coherent thought flees. From his mouth he transfers hunger into my very cells. Every fiber of my being wants him inside me again. He takes his mouth away and I come up heaving for air. They sound like desperate gasps. Sounds I have never heard myself make.

His tongue moves across my collarbone and I whimper. That small mewl of surrender seems to send him into overdrive.

He pushes his knee between my legs and forces them open. Licking the soft swell of my breast and circling his lips around one taut peak, he sucks it softly. I close my eyes and arch back. His large hand skims the soft flesh between my legs. The small bit of lace between us is no match for him. The sound of tearing is loud in my ears.

My eyes fly open and register his as smoldering and intently watching, my face, my mouth, my reactions. His roving fingers encounter thick juices and they make him growl. I stare at him, not understanding it to be the guttural rumble of possession and ownership.

My mouth opens in a silent O, but I do not look away when his fingers first one then two thrust into the wet crease. The thrusting is slow and languorous. Delicious. I raise my body to reach for his mouth. With a groan his hot hungry mouth swoops down to meet mine. As the kiss grows deeper I become lost in the foreign sensations inside me. The blood rushes through my veins and the action between my legs picks up pace, becomes more urgent.

Suddenly he takes his fingers out.

'Don't,' I breathe. My voice is ragged, an unfamiliar mess.

I run my fingers down his hard stomach towards the zip of his pants. My hands are trembling, useless things. He pushes them away gently, and does the job himself.

Naked he is magnificent. A god. Muscles rippling.

He positions himself over me and very slowly sinks his hard flesh into me. He is stretching me, filling me, in a slow, hot movement of pain and shock and… strangely, pleasure…as my sex struggles to accommodate the unfamiliar invasion. His eyes, glazed, the pupils so widely dilated with passion that they are nearly black, never leave me. Watching. Watching. The widening of my own eyes, the way my lips part, the shudders that come to shake my body.

It is sweet torture.

I arch with satisfaction and moan. My soft moans seems to incite him further and he increases the pace of his thrusts. He forces himself deeper and deeper inside me, filling me right to my core.

'Does it still hurt?' he asks.

This deep? Yes. Of course it does. 'No,' I gasp.

So he rocks inside me. Suddenly like a whip passion curls and races through my body, shocking me with its ferocity. It erupts in a strangled cry that surprises even him. He looks at me possessively, proudly, as if he has branded me. He is the owner of my lust. In his hands and mouth and body he holds my pleasure. He said he wanted to fuck me senseless and he does. His pace becomes punishingly hard and fast, but I love the pounding.

Something is billowing through me; it feels as though it could bring some kind of release. When it comes it is a riotous, glorious tidal wave that rips through me. I become one with him, one body, one mind, one soul. But he is still moving. Unfinished.

Then my name tears past his lips. Ah, the tidal wave is upon him.

I come back slowly. The lethargy is
remain spread-eagled in my ecstasy. He gat
limbs gently and shuts them. I look up at hi
He pulls a sheet over my naked skin,
leaves me. The door shuts with its thick clicl

Seventeen

By the time I arrive at the Black Dog, it is heaving with lunchtime trade and Jack is already sitting at a table by a window nursing a pint. As always, the sight of him makes me feel warm inside. I long to run into his arms, he's been fighting my battles for me for as long as I can remember, but this time he can't help.

I make my way through the crowd, many of whom I know, towards him. His straight brown hair is still wet and has been slicked back carelessly. He looks so dear and near and yet so far away from me. He has always been a deeply mysterious person. Hardly anyone really knows him.

He looks up and sees me. He has the pained blue eyes of a tortured artist. He should have been one. He stands slowly, and, unsmiling, opens his arms to me. With a contented sigh, I go into that place where I have felt safest since I was a child. I breathe in the familiar smell of his soap, so clean, so honest. When I pull away, he looks at me carefully. I can tell that he is in a bad mood. Perhaps he is even angry.

'Your hair…'

I smile. 'It'll grow back.'

'No, it's good like that.'

'Yeah?'

Yeah. You all right?'

'Yes.'

'Take a pew and I'll get you a drink. What d'you want?'

'Orange juice.'

He raises his eyebrows. 'And?'

I dimple at him. 'Vodka.'

He nods and makes his way to the bar. I watch him. He is tall and broad-shouldered and Julie Sugar is watching him eagerly. For as long as I can remember Julie has lusted after Jack. And now that he is studying medicine, her desire for him has grown to unmanageable proportions. She catches my eye and waves. I smile and wave back. Immediately, she begins to make her way towards me. I sigh inwardly. I like her, I really do, but I don't want to make small talk today. Besides, she is only coming to talk to me because Jack is here.

'Hey Lana?' she says. She is dressed from head to toe in shades of pink.

'Hi Julie.'

'So Jack's down?' She lays a palm down on the table and drums her fluorescent-pink, plastic nails on it.

'Mmnn.'

'Are you guys having lunch?'

'Probably.'

She looks lingeringly at the empty chair next to me, but I don't invite her to join us. I know Jack will be irritated and besides, I need to talk to Jack and explain.

Jack comes back and stands beside the table with my drink and two packets of salt and vinegar crisps—our favorite flavor.

'Hi, Jack,' Julie simpers up at him, fluttering her eyelashes like a black and white movie star.

Jack smiles tightly. 'Hi.'

'Lana was just telling me that you are about to have lunch. Mind if I join you?' She smiles invitingly.

'Not this time, Jules… We have private things to discuss.'

'Oh.'

'Sorry.'

'Maybe next time then,' she says, and, flashing a hurt smile, flounces off.

'Thanks,' I say, and take my drink off Jack.

Jack sits down and takes a sip of his pint. 'Well, then,' he probes. 'How's it going?'

'Great. No problems,' I say.

His eyes narrow on my face, flash down to my clenched hands, then focus on trying to read my eyes. 'Don't lie to me, Lana. I know you better than that.' His voice becomes hard. 'Has he hurt you?'

'No, course not.'

'Then what is it?' he prompts.

'I'm just confused, I guess. This is not how I thought my life would be.'

'Your life? It's only for a month, isn't it?'

I press my lips together. 'It was three months or no deal.'

Jack draws his breath sharply. 'I wish you hadn't done it, Lana. You never even told me.'

'I knew what you'd say. It was a spur of the moment decision.'

'But to sell yourself.' Jack looks openly angry.

'I'd do it all again, Jack.'

'Yeah, but this treatment you're paying for, it's not even properly recognized. I've looked up this Burzynski character on the net, and he seems well meaning enough, but it's not proper medicine, Lana. All his results are anecdotal. Some of his critics are even accusing him of selling hope.'

I lean forward. 'Do you really think after all these years that the FDA wouldn't have locked him up and thrown away the key if he was just selling hope? Hundreds perhaps thousands of people have been cured by him,' I insist passionately. 'Some people are even calling his method the greatest find of the century.'

'What kind of assurances have they given you?'

'None. In fact, they've already warned me that Mum's chances are slim at best. But even if she has only got a one percent chance of recovery, I'm going to take it. I've got nothing to lose. Everything else has failed. Maybe she'll be one of the lucky ones.'

Jack drops his eyes to the scratched wooden table. 'Remember that time when you were six years old, and I left you outside the newsagent to go in and get some sweets, and when I came out a pervert in a car was trying to persuade you to accept a lift?'

I nod. 'Of course. I remember it as if it was yesterday. Your face, as you came rushing out, and punched the guy through the window. He hit the gas pedal, swerved, nearly hit an oncoming car, and screeched up the road. How old were you then? Fifteen?'

'Yeah. I couldn't believe my eyes. I leave you for one minute to buy some sweets, and you are almost snatched by a pedophile.'

'We didn't tell my mum, did we?'

'No, we didn't. You know what, Lana? It feels like I've just gone into the sweetshop for some sweets and I've come out and a pervert has driven off with you. It feels like I've failed you. I thought I was going to study medicine, get a good job, and be a proper brother to you and your mum. And now it turns out you're out there selling your body.'

'Please don't be angry with me, Jack. I can't bear it when you are.' My eyes well with tears and I blink them away.

His face softens. There is sadness in his voice when he speaks. 'I can't bear it when you cry. I'm not angry with you, Lana. I'm angry with myself for failing you.'

'You haven't failed me, Jack. I'm so proud of you. Of everyone we know, you're the only one who has made it out of this vortex of poverty and hopelessness. I'm not your responsibility. I'm a big girl now. I can take care of myself.'

Jack nods. 'I know. I just wanted better for you.'

'It's not so bad. It's just sex, Jack.'

'How's your mum, anyway?'

'She's bad, Jack. Real bad. The good days are less and less. You do see that I had to do this, don't you?'

'Maybe, but I don't like it, though.'

There is a lull in the conversation and I try to liven it up. 'Since we are openly discussing my sex life…are you gay?'

'What?'

'Are you gay?'

Jack laughs. 'That'll be a surprise to my girlfriend.'

I gasp. 'You have a girlfriend?'

'Mmnnn.'

'Since when?'

'About a week ago. I was always so focused on getting out of the estate I didn't allow myself to get distracted, but my goal is in sight now, and she's a great girl.'

'And just when were you going to tell me, Jack Irish?'

'Well, how could I with you springing your big news on me?'

'Tell me more about her.'

Before he can answer, my phone rings. It is Blake. 'Hi,' I say, looking at Jack.

'Are you at the apartment?'

'No.'

'Can you get there in thirty minutes?'

'I guess so.'

'See you in thirty minutes.'

'That was him?' Jack asks.

I nod. 'I've got to go. I'll take a rain check on lunch with you, but I'm buying and we're going somewhere nice.'

'With his money?'

I don't say anything. Of course it's his money. My credit cards were maxed out before him.

'Thanks, but no thanks. I understand why you're doing what you're doing, but I'll be damned if I'm going to help spend his money. As far as I'm concerned it's blood money—your blood. I'm not going to drink from it.'

I look at him helplessly. 'It's not that bad. Don't let it come between us, please,' I beg.

He reaches forward and grasps my hands in his. 'Nothing will come between us. I'll always be here for you and will be long after he is gone. No matter what happens, I want you to know I'm always here, a phone call away. You can always come to me.'

Tears spring into my eyes. 'What's the name of that girlfriend of yours?' I sniff.

'Alison.'

'She's lucky.'

He smiles. 'You must tell her.'

'When?'

'You'll see at Jerry's birthday party. I'm bringing her.'

I bite my lip. 'If I am allowed to be there, I would love to meet her.'

His eyes narrow dangerously. 'Are you some kind of sexual slave to him, Lana?'

I feel hot color run up my neck. 'No, but it's the arrangement—I have to be there whenever he wants me.'

Jack draws a sharp breath. 'That is just sick,' he fumes.

I cover my burning cheeks with my palms. 'Please, Jack, leave it.'

'You're such a fucking innocent. Does your mother know about this pact of abuse you have signed up for?'

'Of course she doesn't, but it's not abuse, Jack. It's not exactly a hardship to sleep with the man that *Hello*! magazine has called the most eligible bachelor in the world.'

'So what *does* your mother think?'

I close my eyes. 'She thinks I've got myself a rich boyfriend.'

'Jesus.'

I run a finger through the condensation on my glass. 'You know I don't believe in God. All my life I've thought it's a cruel God up there, if there is one at all, but you do, and your God is kind and forgiving. Will you pray to your god to save my mother?'

'I pray every day for your mum, Lana.'

Tears spill down my cheeks.

Sadly, he reaches out a hand and wipes them. 'Don't cry, little one. Maybe this treatment will work. Maybe she will get better.'

I smile through my tears. 'I don't know what I'd do without you, Jack. Sometimes when I am really sad I think of you studying in your dorm, and it makes me feel happy. "Dr Jack Irish, your next patient has arrived."'

Jack smiles, but it is a sad smile.

'I did what I had to do.'

He rests his forehead on his hand; his eyes are unexpectedly gentle. 'All right, Lana. We'll play it your way. Be safe and remember I'm here for you. Always. If ever it gets…strange or dangerous, call me immediately. I swear if he ever hurts you, I don't care if I end up in prison, I'm going to punch his lights out.'

I nod. 'I'll be all right. It's just sex,' I say and he winces.

'Please don't say that again, Lana. It hurts my ears.'

'I've not suddenly become Fat Mary, you know.'

'Perish the thought,' Jack says, the ghost of a smile flickering into his face.

'I have to go now.'

He stands. 'I'll pop by and see your mum later.'

'Thanks Jack. She'll like that. She likes you. Do you know she thought you and I would get together?'

He makes a face. 'Oh dear.'

I laugh. 'I know. Goodbye, Jack.'

I move forward, kiss him on his cheek and walk towards the entrance. As I cross it my phone flashes with an incoming text.

Wear nothing.

I look at the screen again. *Wear nothing.* And feel a stirring of excitement deep in my core.

Eighteen

In the bathroom mirror my eyes seem almost smoky. I undress quickly and pull on the bathrobe hanging behind the door. I still haven't got used to my hairless body. It seems too girlish, somehow, but I think I know why he wants it so. Everything in his life is neat and tidy. Not a pubic hair out of place.

When I hear him in the corridor I freeze.

Wear nothing.

I take the bathrobe off, slip into the bedroom and stand inside the door. He is already there dressed in dark gray trousers and white shirt. His tie is loosened and his shirtsleeves have been haphazardly folded up his muscular arms. His watch glints against his tan. He comes to me and leads me to the big black armchair by the large mirror. I see myself in the mirror. Nude.

Fully clothed he stands behind me.

'Porcelain skin and fuck me now, blue eyes. How beautiful you are,' he says, watching me through the mirror. His eyes are heavy-lidded and cloudy with desire.

He hooks his handmade leather shoe underneath my right foot and gently lifts it. The leather is cool and smooth and the laces rub erotically against the soft sole of my foot. His shoe deposits my foot on the padded seat of the big black chair.

The position has exposed my sex in the most indecent way. I don't recognize the woman in the mirror. She looks wanton and shameless. Now I know the real reason why I am bald. There is nothing to hide behind.

It is all so shameful it is exciting. I look away.

'I want you to see what I am doing to you.'

I meet his eyes in the mirror. He kisses my neck and I moan and try to turn towards him.

'No, watch.'

Throbbing with excitement I gaze at the mirror. I have willingly spread open my sex and allowed him access into my most intimate part. I feel his fully clothed body brush against me. Vaguely: buttons pressing into my back…soft wool against my buttocks and thighs.

'I love your skin. It is like the finest silk.'

Then his hand is moving towards my navel and sliding downwards without any resistance. All the while he is watching me watch myself.

His palm comes to press on my pubic bone and I watch the palm make circles. The circles become tighter and tighter until they are moving the flesh over my clit. Suddenly his index finger taps on the nub and I shiver with helpless wanting.

'Not yet,' he whispers. 'I will decide when you come.'

Then his fingers move quickly in a sweeping motion along my crack, gathering juice. There is more than enough there. The lubricated finger circles the swollen, throbbing bud. Watching him pleasure me is the most unexpectedly erotic thing I have experienced.

I draw a sharp breath and long for the feeling of being full. That feeling of having him inside me, but he does not give that to me. Instead he rubs around my sex, his fingers are cunningly methodical. The same movement again and again.

In minutes I feel the waves coming, but as I push eagerly towards them, towards release, his fingers stop, and even though I press my hips towards them, they stubbornly refuse to move, until the waves dissipate. I sag against him, frustrated, and he slowly pushes his finger into me.

'Wet, hot and tight,' he murmurs.

I look at his large hand; the thick, masculine wrist peppered with silky hair working me. Again that longing to be filled, not with one finger, but with the magnificently thick, long shaft inside his trousers. I have to bite my lip to stop myself from crying out, Fuck me.

'Kiss me,' he orders.

I twist my neck around and give him my mouth. His tongue enters it. I suck greedily. A finger becomes two and increases speed. Just as I am beginning to enjoy the rhythm the fingers are withdrawing, slipping and sliding around the lips. He takes his mouth away as his other hand leaves my waist and cupping my chin, holds it facing the mirror.

I stare at myself in shock. At his big hand moving and the glistening redness of my engorged sex—it is as if it is alive. A shameless greedy creature. And suddenly I am coming and… hard. Real hard. I open my mouth in a shout as my knees buckle and I feel myself losing balance. His hand tightens like a vice around my waist.

When it is over I lean my head back against his chest for a moment.

'Hold onto the chair,' he says, and bends me over. He puts a hand on my back at waist level and pushes down, so my hips are angled, my sex is more exposed. I hear his zip and the soft sound of his trousers dropping. Putting his palm on either side of my face he turns my head and makes me watch what he is doing to me.

'I want you to watch me fucking you.'

With wild eyes I look at the image our bodies make as he grabs me by the hips and his proud cock disappears inside me.

'Now, let me hear your cries. Purr for me, Lana,' he commands and rams ferociously into my willing, dripping wetness.

I cry out with the sensations: the fullness and the depths that he has gone into.

It is surprisingly painful, but such is my need to have him inside that I welcome the pain and push back against him, to take more of him. So he goes even deeper, until his thick shaft is buried all the way to the root. I grunt inelegantly. One hand falls on my back, pushing me into the armchair, while the other grasps my shoulder.

'Ah.'

Suddenly, the animal in him takes over. With bestial urgency he drives into me. Harder and faster. Grinding me against him. The solid armchair rocks with his thrusts. And at that moment I am utterly possessed by the man. His to do anything with.

As he slams into me I realize that the palm of his hand that is pressed against my pubic bone is bringing forth different sensations. The rubbing is causing me to crest again. It is explosive this time, it makes my body convulse uncontrollably and lasts, even past his last urgent thrusts and his own groan of release.

I feel his body slacken against mine. With both his arms around my waist he straightens me, and holds me close to him while he is still inside. I look at him in the mirror and find his eyes unreadable.

Wordlessly, he withdraws out of me and goes into the bathroom.

Without him in the mirror I seem alone and abandoned. On trembling legs I move to hide my nakedness inside the bathrobe.

Nineteen

I am so anxious about my mother meeting Blake that I forget to warn Blake of her wasted appearance. It is only when she opens the door in her best blue dress, a new blue scarf, and smiling through freshly applied lipstick that I realize what she must look like to a stranger. But when I look up at Blake he is smiling and suave. He hands my mother the bouquet of flowers he has brought for her and steps through the door into our home.

'Thank you for inviting me, Mrs. Bloom. It is a great pleasure to finally meet you.'

'Nice to meet you too, Mr. Barrington.'

'Please, you must call me Blake.'

'And you must call me Nys.'

'Nys? Ah…French.'

'Yes, not many people know that. My mother loved the sound of it.'

'I agree with her. A pretty name it is,' he charms.

'Come in, come in,' my mother invites.

Blake takes my hand. I am surprised at how casually he does it. As if he has done it many times before. My mother has decorated the table with fresh flowers and candles. The door to the small balcony is open and the sound of children swearing floats up. My mother quickly closes the door and puts on some music instead.

'Something smells very good,' Blake says.

Mother glows with pleasure. It is obvious she is taken with Blake. 'Oh, it's just chicken and rice. A Persian recipe.'

'With fruit?'

'Yes, pomegranates. How did you know?'

And so the night goes with my mother glowing and impressed and Blake urbane and genteel.

When the food appears it is delicious. Blake makes it a point to polish his plate. Occasionally, he looks with adoring eyes at me, and other times reaches for my hand, never too obvious, and so real it makes me freeze uncomfortably. Once he even reaches forward and lightly brushes his lips against mine. I blink with surprise and glance at my mother, but she is smiling happily at me. Another time he looks mockingly into my eyes as he strokes the inside of my wrist. I turn away in confusion.

This Blake I cannot understand or deal with. This Blake is dangerous to my well-being.

This Blake I would want to keep beyond the three months stipulation.

For dessert mother serves a chocolate melt in the middle pudding. Again, Blake makes it a point to finish every last drop. When my mother offers him a strong, Middle Eastern coffee, he immediately accepts.

There is only one uncomfortable moment in the evening when my mother turns to Blake and asks, 'Have you ever done anything that you wish you could go back and undo? Something you regret?'

'No,' Blake says easily.

My mother turns to me. 'What about you, Lana?'

I look my mother in the eye. 'Absolutely not.'

We sit in the back of the Bentley with Tom driving.

'How is it you know so much about Persian history?'

'It was part of our school curriculum.'

'I don't remember learning anything like that in school.'

'That is because you were right in what you said yesterday. My education has been designed to make me a leader, and yours to turn you into an obedient worker. It is how a capitalist system works. No country can be successful without its workers.'

'But is it right?'

Blake turns away from me and stares out of the window.

For a while neither of us speak, then Blake turns towards me. 'You needed the money for her, didn't you?'

'To send her to America for treatment. She leaves tomorrow.'

'Where is she going?'

'The Burzynsky Research Center.'

'I have heard of Dr. Burzynsky. The FDA have taken him to court a few times and not been able to indict him. A good sign for your mother.' In the dark his eyes stare at me with an expression I cannot comprehend.

When we reach the apartment, he drops the key onto the side table. 'Want a nightcap?'

'OK.'

We go into the living room with its low lights. 'What will you have?'

'Baileys.'

I go to the long sofa and watch him pour me a drink, drop some ice cubes into it, and then pour himself a finger of Scotch. He stands over me and holds my drink out to me. I take it and he eases himself beside me.

'Would you like to go shopping with Fleur again tomorrow?'

'No.'

He turns to look at me. 'Why not?'

I shrug. 'I've still got things I haven't worn yet. Besides, I'd like to spend some time with my mum before she leaves in the evening.'

He nods. 'What kind of cancer?'

'It is in her lungs, liver, femur bone and pelvis.'

There is a flash of something in his eyes. He does not believe my mother will make it. He drops his eyes to his drink. He takes a sip, puts it down on the glass table.

'Come here,' he says.

I scoot closer, but he lifts me bodily by the waist while I squeal, and puts me so I am sitting astride him. My open pussy comes in contact with the bulge in his trousers. I stop laughing. I can feel myself becoming wet. I bend forward and run my tongue along his ear. When I reach his earlobe I take it between my teeth and nibble.

'Hey,' he says suddenly, and pulls me away from him.

I look at him surprised.

‘Where did that come from?’ he asks.

‘My best friend Billie taught me the technique, but I probably did it wrong. Did I bite too hard or something?’

‘Or something.’ He rubs my plump lower lip absently. ‘I can’t believe an innocent like you still exists.’ He lifts his eyes to mine. ‘Here, let me show you a much more useful technique.’

And that night, he unzips his trousers and teaches me how to take his silky cock entwined by its two angry green veins and pleasure him with my mouth.

I awaken in the dark and know immediately that I am not alone. For the first time, he has stayed the night with me. I feel the heat from his body and listen to his deep, even breathing. Carefully, I ease my body away from his and as silently as possible grope across the surface of my bedside table. I find the remote control and switch on the bathroom light.

Light filters through the half closed door and dimly illuminates his face. I turn my head and for a long time simply watch him asleep on his side, facing me. The lines that hold his face so tightly during the day are relaxed and soft. Like this, he is heartbreakingly beautiful. I have an irrational desire to run my index finger along his stubby eyelashes. I don’t. Instead, I slip out of bed and throwing a large T-shirt over my head, make for the light.

I close the door behind me, use the toilet and wait for its quiet whirling to end before I open the door. My trip to my side of the bed is interrupted by the sight of his wallet lying on his bedside cabinet. I stop and look at it. Once, when I was very young, I opened my father’s wallet to look inside and was saddened by what I found inside. Two five pound notes, the coin purse bulging with small change, a petrol receipt, and no photographs of either my mother or me.

I had taken it to my nose and sniffed it. Many years after he left us, I would come across other men's wallets and wonder what they kept inside theirs. I find myself moving towards Blake's wallet. As my fingers connect with the expensive hide, a steely hand clamps down on mine. I gasp with shock and land on the bed beside him, my startled eyes flying to his face. His are alert and watching.

'What are you doing?'

'Nothing,' I say lamely, my face flaming.

'Ask if you need money.' His voice is cold and distant.

Only then it occurs to me what it must look like to him. I shake my head in horror. 'I wasn't trying to steal your money. I just wanted to see what was in it.'

For a moment he looks at me curiously, almost the way a dog will tilt its head when it is trying to figure out what you are trying to communicate to it. Then he takes the wallet and tosses it into my lap. 'So look.' His eyes move to my mouth as my teeth worry at my lower lip.

'What? With you watching?'

His eyebrows rise. 'Would that spoil the…er… experience?'

I swallow, sit up and open the wallet. It is slimmer than my father's, the leather wonderfully soft. And it smells new. There are no photographs behind the plastic of his wallet either, only the deep red card that it came with. I run my thumb along the stitching and down the credit card sleeves. There are only five cards in it, none of them from high street banks. One seems to be from Coutts, another is an American Express Black, and the other three I do not recognize. There is a wad of fifty-pound notes that have the look and feel of freshly-minted money. No small change at all in the purse section. I close it and return it to the bedside.

'Well?'

'You wouldn't understand.'

'Do you know that you're one strange girl?'

I look down at my bare feet and wriggle my toes. 'Have you never wanted to look in a woman's handbag?'

'Never.'

'Why not?'

He rubs his chin. 'Can't say the contents of a woman's handbag have ever held any interest for me. I was always more interested in the contents of their clothes.'

With a sigh, I get up to return to my side.

'Like now,' he says softly.

I look down on him, a half smile on my face, before I pull the T-shirt over my head and discard it on the floor.

His eyes begin to glitter, and instantly my body responds and yearns for him. The tug of anticipation is strong, but I don't go to him. I stand very still as the juices accumulate between my thighs.

'Come here,' he says finally, his voice at once husky and slumberous, and it is a relief to have that man's strong hands grasp me by my upper arms and press me into the mattress.

Twenty

I wake up early, and press the remote button for the curtains. They sweep open, revealing a beautiful day. The sun is already shining brightly. I dress quickly in a pair of old jeans and a T-shirt and head for the coffee machine. After several tries I walk to the phone and call the desk downstairs.

Mr. Nair answers and immediately tells me he will be around to show me how to use it. Less than five minutes later he is at my door. He even shows me how to froth the milk for my cappuccino. He explains that he used to work in a coffee bar in his younger days.

'Do you want one?' I offer.

Mr. Nair's eyes shine. 'Are you sure, Miss Bloom? We only have instant downstairs and I'd love a real coffee.'

'Of course I'm sure,' I say and take down another saucer and cup.

'Ah,' Mr. Nair says delicately. 'I am a Brahmin and I am not allowed to drink from other people's cups. I have my own mug. I will bring it up.'

And he does. He brings his own I Am The Boss mug, and I open a tin of biscuits and offer it to him. He takes two. I raise a that's-it eyebrow, and he grins and helps himself to two more.

'Any time you want a real coffee, call me, and if I am in, feel free to come up,' I say.

'Thank you. Thank you, Miss Bloom, you are very kind indeed.'

After coffee I go to my mother's house. We have a busy day ahead. We pick up her wig from Selfridges and spend some time shopping for things she will need. My mother chooses a burgundy trouser-suit that looks very good on her, two pretty pastel dresses, and some new underwear. Afterwards, I watch while two women give her a pedicure and manicure. They paint her nails coral.

My mother smiles at them shyly when they tell her she has beautiful hands.

Afterwards, we take a quick trip to the doctor's surgery. We spend the rest of the afternoon at the flat. By five the flat is clean and my mother is ready. She stands before me in the living room in her burgundy trouser-suit and her new wig. She looks wonderful.

I cry. So does my mother.

Billie shoos us both out of the flat. I watch my mother and Billie get into a mini cab and head for Heathrow. Then I go back to our empty home, fall on my mother's bed and cry my heart out. It is nearly six when I wash my face and leave for the apartment.

I am surprised to see that Blake is already in. He comes out of the dining room when he hears me.

'Has she gone?'

I nod, feeling very distant from him.

'That's good. I thought you might not feel like going out tonight so perhaps we can have a Chinese takeaway?'

'Not for me.'

'Don't you want any food?'

I shake my head.

'Would you like to lie down and rest for a bit?'

'Yes. That's a good idea.'

'OK, sleep for a bit. It'll do you good.'

I nod and he retreats into the dining room. As I pass him in the corridor, I notice his briefcase is open and there are papers spread out on the long dining table, and he appears to be concentrating hard on them.

I lie down on the bed and fall asleep almost immediately. My sleep is restless and full of dreams. A noise wakes me in the middle of the night. I realize instantly that I am alone in bed. I listen again. It is coming from the kitchen. The little bedside clock says it is two a.m. My mother and Billie will still be in the air. I get out of bed, and pad towards the sounds.

I stand at the doorway dazzled by the light, pushing hair away from my eyes. Blake is toasting two slices of bread and does not see me. My mind takes a picture of him—gorgeously shirtless and wearing only his low-slung jeans—to be kept for later, when he is no longer around. When he spots me, he leans a hip against the work counter, and looks at me, his arms crossed, his eyes unreadable.

'Did I wake you?'

'No. What are you making?'

'I was working and I got hungry. Want some toast?'

I shake my head, but come into the room and sit on a stool. I put my elbows on the island surface amongst the butter dish, knives, plates and open jars of foie gras and caviar. There is also a half-drunk glass of orange juice. I slide my body along the cold granite surface and pull it over to me. As I sip at it I watch him work.

He produces a spoon from a drawer. It is the smallest spoon I have seen. He scoops a tiny amount of caviar and holds it out to me.

I crinkle my nose. 'Fish eggs?'

He shakes his head in disgust. 'Philistine,' he chides.

I open my mouth and he inserts the spoon. Little salty balls explode intriguingly in my mouth.

'Good?'

I smile. 'Tastes better than it looks. A bit like you,' I tease.

He throws back his head and laughs.

'You work very hard, don't you?'

'All rich people do.'

I watch him spread pâtè on a slice of toast. Watch his even, strong teeth bite cleanly into it.

'You should eat something,' he says.

I stand up and make myself a jam sandwich. While I am eating it, I think Rosa was right. Jam sandwiches should be made with white bread. They simply don't taste the same with healthy bread.

'What do you feel like doing now?' he asks.

'Don't you feel like sleeping?'

'Eventually.'

'Shall we play a game?'

A smile curves that straight mouth. 'What kind of game?'

'Let's see who climaxes first.'

His eyes flash. 'What are the rules?'

Hmm… Billie didn't mention anything about rules. 'It's quite a simple game really. We take turns to make each other come. We time ourselves with an egg timer. The one who lasts the longest at the hands of the other wins.'

'What's the prize for winning?'

'The winner gets to ask the loser for anything they want?'

'What if the loser is unable to provide that thing?'

'Within reason and nothing dangerous, obviously.'

'OK, do you want to go first? Or shall I?'

'I will. You can do me first.' I stand up and swipe the egg timer off the counter. He stares at me as if he is unable to understand me. We go into the bedroom and it is easy for him to make me come. Then it is my turn.

'Why did you let me win?' I whisper.

'How do you know I did?'

'Because you've never come before me.'

'So why did you want to play this game then?'

'Because I had something special up my sleeve, but I didn't even get a chance to use it.'

He laughs. 'Something special? Is it another technique from Billie?'

'As a matter of fact, yes, but you haven't answered the original question.'

'Because I wanted to know what you would ask for.'

'Why?'

He shrugs. 'Well, what do you want?'

'I want you to cook for me.'

He lies on his side and props his head on his palm. 'Why?'

'When I was fourteen, I read a book where the hero sent the heroine to have a long soak in the bath while he cooked for her. He grilled two steaks and tossed a salad. It was really romantic. He wore a black shirt and washed out blue jeans. I remember he had just had a shower and his hair was still wet. Oh, and he was barefoot.'

'And what did the heroine wear?'

'Er… I can't remember.'

'Dinner tomorrow?'

I smile. 'Dinner tomorrow. You won't burn it, will you?'

'Maybe just the salad.'

Twenty one

The next day drags slowly. Mr. Nair stops by at ten a.m. with his mug. We have a little chat and he tells me about his family in India. Before he worked in the coffee shop, he was a Hindu priest in a temple in India. He is interesting, but his break time is quickly over and he leaves.

I am required to idle away my days, but idling alone in a sumptuous flat, I am quickly realizing, is no easy thing. There is not much activity in the part of the park that my balcony faces, and daytime television has always bored me. How many times can one watch reruns of *Wonder Woman*?

I am also terribly lonely. Without my mother, Billie or Jack I feel quite lost. I wander around the large flat alone and bored. Idling, I finally decide, requires thoughtful planning and effort—diligent effort. I begin by ordering some books from Amazon.

It is nearly five o'clock when I am able to Skype Billie. I sit cross-legged on the bed and look at Billie's dear, excited face come alive on the screen.

'Guess what?' Billie shouts enthusiastically. 'We flew first class.'

'What?'

'Yep, we arrived at economy check-in and we were bumped up to first class. Both your mum and me!'

'How can that be?'

'Must be banker boy. They said it was all arranged and paid for.'

I am speechless. Could it really have been Blake who paid the difference? But he didn't even know which flight they were on.

'Anyway,' Billie says, 'it was bloody brilliant. They called us by name and acted like we were celebrities or something. I drank nearly two bottles of champagne, and your mum got to sleep most of the way.'

'How is mum?'

'She's here. I'll put her on.'

'Hello, Lana,' my mother says shakily. She looks so white and fragile that I almost burst into tears. When the call is over I lie on the bed and wonder why Blake did that. He is a strange man. So cold and distant sometimes and so incredibly kind and generous at other times.

At seven o'clock, Blake arrives. I run out to meet him at the front door.

'Did you pay for my mum and Billie to fly first class?'

'Yes.'

'Why?'

He shrugs casually. 'I like your mother,' he says shortly, and sends me into the Jacuzzi bath.

'Dinner is at seven thirty sharp,' he says. 'Don't come out before.'

I climb into it and close my eyes. It is heaven. Blake comes in with a glass of red wine.

'To get you in the mood,' he says.

'This is not in the scene, but impressive improvisation,' I say as I accept it.

I take a sip and open Philip K. Dick's *Do Androids Dream of Electric Sheep*. Fifteen minutes later, I smell it. Burning. Before I can wrap myself in the toweling robe, the fire alarms go off. I rush to the kitchen dripping soapsuds.

Blake has opened all the windows, and is standing on a chair desperately waving a magazine at the smoke detector in the corridor. His hair is slightly wet, he is wearing a black shirt with two buttons undone, and a pair of stone washed jeans. He is also barefoot.

I begin to laugh. 'Did you burn the salad?' I shout above the racket.

He scowls down at me.

I go into the kitchen and bin the blackened pieces of meat. Shaking my head, I pop a piece of tomato from the salad into my mouth, and immediately spit it out. Mega salty. The salad goes the way of the steaks. The alarm finally stops blaring. I look up and he is standing at the doorway.

'You've never cooked, have you?'

'No,' he confesses. 'Do you want to go out?'

'Why don't we just have some chip butties instead?'

'Chip butties?'

'Oh. My. God. You've never had a chip butty? You don't know what you're missing. You have to have one.'

'OK.'

'Let me get ready and I'll pop over to the shop and get the ingredients.'

'I'll come with you,' he offers.

We walk together to the local fish and chip shop where I order a big bag of chips.

'No fish?'

'No fish. Now we need to go into the corner shop for some bread.'

'Don't we have some back at the flat?'

'Nah. We've got the good stuff back there. This is poor people's food. For this we need a loaf of cheap, white bread.'

I pick out a loaf of sliced white bread and Blake pays for it.

'That's it,' I say.

'Are those *all* the ingredients you need for our meal?'

'The rest we have at home,' I say, and with horror realize what I have said. I called the flat home. But he says nothing and I just hope he did not notice.

In the kitchen, Blake sits on the counter and watches me liberally butter four slices of bread, load two up with chips, squirt tomato ketchup in a zigzag pattern over them, sprinkle salt, and close them into two chunky sandwiches.

'Voilà. The famous chip butty.'

'That's it?'

I push a plate towards him. 'Taste it.'

He eyes it without desire.

'Go on. I tasted caviar for you.'

'That's true.' He takes a tiny bite and begins to chew cautiously.

'No, no, that's not how you eat it. You have to attack it. Like this.' I open my mouth and take a huge bite. He follows suit. It is strange watching him eat with such abandon.

'Well?' I demand.

'Not bad actually. Kind of satisfying.'

'This is what a lot of kids on the estate live on most of the time.'

'Did you?'

'No, my mother never had a drinking or a drug problem so she didn't have to dip into our food money to finance her habit.'

'Did you have a happy childhood?'

'Yeah, I guess so. Until my mother got sick I was very happy.'

'How come you never had a boyfriend?'

I wipe my lips on a paper napkin, swallow, and grin. 'All the boys were scared of Jack. And after my mother got sick and my father left, any thoughts of boys were gone.'

'Who's Jack?'

'He's the closest thing I have to a brother.'

'Why were they scared of him?'

'Because Jack was not only big and strong, he was also utterly fearless. When we were growing up there was nobody he was scared of. Everybody knew Jack had taken me under his wing, and nobody wanted to mess with him. Once Billie, Leticia, Jack and me went to a club, and a guy there wanted to dance with me. He wouldn't take no for an answer so Jack said, "You heard her. Now scram." Of course, he didn't take that too good so he waited with his mates for us outside the club.'

I stop to pop a fat chip into my mouth.

'And surrounded us. One of them had a knife. I was so frightened. I remember Jack looked at me and said,

"Shhh… you know I got ya," and then he smiled. That Jack smile. And I knew it would be all right. I walked out of the circle and they closed in on him. I can still see them now. Tattoos, broken teeth, rings where there should be none. But what shocked me was Jack. He was like a stranger. I couldn't recognize him.

'All those years I thought I knew him, warm and friendly, an unshakeable rock, and suddenly I see this fiend turning on himself, snarling, "Come on then. Who's first?" They advanced in a group. He kicked the one with the knife in the throat and another he punched in the nose, bled like crazy. Then he felled another two guys, I don't know how, it happened so fast, and then it was over. The last coward ran away. It was like watching a movie. And you know what the first thing Jack said to me was? "Are *you* all right?"'

'Unusual guy,' Blake says quietly. 'Did you never want to go out with him?'

'No, he is my brother. My safe harbor. I'd do anything for him.'

He nods. There is no expression in his face. 'How long has your mother been ill?' he asks, and takes another bite of his sandwich.

'Just before I turned fifteen. And that was also when my dad left. I was so scared she was going to die. If not for Jack, I don't know how things would have turned out. He came around every day and did what my father should have done.'

'And you've never seen your dad since he left?'

I shake my head.

'Did you not want to?'

'No. I heard he married again and had more kids, but he really doesn't interest me anymore. He ran out on us. He thought my mother would die and he would be saddled with me.'

'Hmmm... You've never had an orgasm until you met me, have you?'

I am certain my face must be astonishingly red. 'Was it that obvious?'

'A bit. You never had a boyfriend but you must have masturbated while growing up.'

'You don't know what my life was like. For most of my life I've been terrified of losing my mother. Whenever she was ill, I slept with her. And when she was not—which was not often, and I returned to my own bed I could never do anything—my mother is such a light sleeper. She will wake up if a pin drops.'

Blake takes his last bite and pushes away from the stool. 'Got some work to do. Can you amuse yourself for a bit and meet me in an hour's time in the bedroom?'

'OK.'

In the bedroom I reach for his trousers. I want to give him pleasure the way he taught me.

'Easy, tiger,' he says and spreads my legs. Watching me intently he latches onto my clit covered in its juices and begins to gently suck it. The sensation is indescribable—delicate ribbons of pleasure rise from his mouth and enter my being. I tremble against his mouth. I forget to think and become an extension of my sex, my core. He is teaching my sex, what it can be. Soon my nails become claws that dig into his shoulders. My mouth opens and my muscles begin to contract with anticipation of the explosion that is coming.

But when he judges the train wreck is almost upon me he deliberately slows his movement, brings me back down only to begin again on that velvet-soft swollen flesh. His eyes monitor my reaction. Again and again until I am holding his head in my hands and begging him to let me climax.

'I can't take it anymore,' I plead.

And this time he relents. He lets me come and it shocks me by its intensity. I scream his name, but strangely, he refuses to take his mouth away from my painfully sensitive blood-engorged sex. I try to wriggle away but his grip is steel. Then, suddenly I am no longer pushing his head away and begging him to stop, but pulling him back in; the waves of ecstasy are coming back. And again. Three times in total I jerk, shake, tremble and soar before I fall from my great height.

My hands flop to my sides, spent.

I feel him take his watching eyes away from me and lay his cheek for a moment on my stomach and listen to my ragged breathing.

Then he bounds up, full of coiled energy and picking me up lays me on the pillow. I am so spent I look at him with hazy, passion-filled eyes. I want to tell him that I have never experienced such a thing before. I want to tell him how beautiful and awesome it has been, how complete he has made me feel; perhaps I might even have blurted out that I am in love with him and have been for some time now.

There is no one but him for me—I would take the bad, the good, even the indifferent—but he places a silencing finger on my lips. He does not want words from me. He wants only claim of my body and only when he wants it.

All he was doing was defining me as his. As my eyes flutter shut I hear him step out of his trousers and feel the mattress give under his knee.

Ah, it's not over yet.

Twenty two

Blake Law Barrington

It is late, nearly twelve, when I slot my key in the door and enter the apartment. The sliding doors to the balcony are open and a gentle breeze plays with the curtain. I see her asleep on the sofa and feel a frisson of some strange emotion. I stand over her and watch her.

In the soft light, the pattern on the lavender wallpaper looks like thorn vines that the prince from *Sleeping Beauty* has to hack through. I can still remember reading it for my sister. So many times. It was her favorite. I fucking hated it. Corny nonsense. I sit next to her and her sleeping body tilts twenty degrees towards me. I run a finger along her cheek and she opens her eyes.

'You smell of whiskey. Where have you been?'

I chuckle. 'Doing my rounds.'

She puts a hand to my cheek. 'You're cold.' She moves the hand to my chest. Through the shirt material, her fingertips register the beat of my heart.

'You reminded me of Sleeping Beauty.'

'That must make you Prince Charming then.'

A cloud of sadness settles in my chest. My hand gently traces the line of her cheek. 'Don't deceive yourself, Lana. Our liaison can only ever be temporary. I am spoken for.'

My words stab her like a knife. I see the pain spread through her eyes. Her wounds are whispers. 'Who is she? Where is she now?'

'She's from an old family like me. She has to finish her education. She is only twenty-two. Next year I will be thirty-one and she will be twenty-three. Then we will marry.'

'Are you in love with her?'

The thought is almost amusing. 'No.'

'Is it like an arranged marriage?'

'Something like that. There is some leeway, there has to be some attraction, but marriage for us has always been a merger of two great families. The Lazards marry their sons to Rockefellers and the Rockefellers marry their daughters to Hapsgoods. It works well.'

'Is love ever a part of the equation?'

'Love is vastly overrated. We consolidate our wealth and position and make arrangements to cater to our specific tastes.'

'Specific tastes?'

'Some of us are gay; others are pedophiles.'

She looks at me in shock. 'Are you condoning pedophilia?'

'I'm not condoning anything. I'm stating a fact.'

'So you wouldn't report a pedophile who was abusing a child?'

I shake my head. 'That is a matter between the pedophile and God as God made him that way.'

'What about the child?' she demands.

'Time's march is a web of causes and effects, and asking for any gift of mercy, however tiny it might be, is to ask that a link be broken in that web of iron. No one deserves such a miracle—Jorge Luis Borges.'

'What an unkind world you live in.'

'Your tragedy is that you live in the same world as me only you do not perceive it, and that makes you careless.'

'And your tragedy is your fatalism.'

'On the contrary. It means I recognize the threat. Cause and effect. Unlike you, my wife and I will guard our children in such a way that they will never be exposed to dangerous situations.'

She gazes at me with horror at the calm and shamelessly way I discuss my bride to be with her. 'If you are already engaged to be married why are you never seen together and why are you being touted as the most eligible bachelor alive?'

'You will never understand us. Don't try.'

'Is it the same reason your family doesn't appear in the Forbes rich list?'

My lips curve. 'That's better. Now you are beginning to understand. The greatest fortunes are all secretly earned, ferociously guarded.'

'So… You are the most eligible bachelor because…'

'The impression of meritocracy must be maintained at all times.'

'Ah, the taint of elitism.'

'No, but close.'

'Why so evasive? I am bound by contract. I couldn't speak even if I wanted to.'

'If you controlled eighty percent of all the wealth in the world… Wouldn't you want the status quo to carry on? We prefer to trade anonymously behind a façade, behind the public faces. Kings, prime ministers, tsars, sultans, and emperors come to power and lose it to the jealously and dissatisfaction of the people. We have, uninterrupted, ruled from behind the scenes for centuries. Our secrets are precious.'

'What time is it?' She sounds defeated.

'Time you were in bed,' I say, and lift her into my arms. Her hands go around my neck.

'You're getting long, Bloom.'

'Too long for you, Barrington.'

'Never too long for me, Bloom.'

She turns her head and sees our reflections in the mirror on the opposite wall. Her long nightgown trails behind her and in the soft light from the nightstand she really does seem like a princess in need of rescuing.

'We look like the romantic hero and heroine of the black and white movies my mother likes to watch.'

I don't say anything.

'Only we are not,' she adds sadly. 'All your plans don't include me.'

The thought is depressing. It makes me feel sad when she buries her face in my neck.

'To sleep?' she whispers.

'Not quite, Bloom,' I reply quietly.

I drop her in the bed with a plop and look down at her tousled hair on the white pillows. In the shadows her eyes are unreadable.

'What is it?' she asks.

I bring my mouth towards her and her mouth lifts to meet me. This time our kiss is special. I feel myself heat up at the answering purr of her body. It is as though we are drinking from each other. Our bodies meld together.

And when we are lying sated in the dark I become fearful of her and have to spoil it. 'I love it when you come and your pussy grips my cock.'

She shuts her eyes and turns her face away from me in despair. She understands what I am doing.

Always, she must be reduced to an orifice.

Twenty three

Lana Bloom

Today, I feel happy. Billie called to tell me the good news. The antineoplastons that my mother is on are working. The tests are back—the tumors are regressing. My mother will have to carry on her treatment for another three months, but she can return in two days' time to England and carry it on here.

I am so happy I start sobbing.

To celebrate, Blake takes me out to dinner at Le Gavroche. I have already dined on the most delicious cheese soufflé cooked in double cream followed by grilled scallops, and my dessert, a raspberry millefeuille in praline-flavored chocolate, has just been put in front of me.

Blake has ordered the Le Plateau de Fromages Affines and I watch him cut a slice of strong cheese. It is almost transparently thin. He places it on a small square of cracker and slips it into his mouth. I imagine the flavors building up in his nose, the cheese melting on his hot, silky tongue, and cheesy liquids traveling down the back of his throat. I watch the movement in the strong column of his brown throat. The entire operation is fluid, elegant, almost a ceremony. It is his education. There is no greed in him.

Not even for me.

I look away and meet the eyes of another diner, a man. He is looking at me with the same expression I must have had in my face while I was looking at the banker. Now I know what lies in the belly of all those men who have ever gazed at me with desire in their eyes. I look down at my dessert, dip my finger into the praline-flavored chocolate and place it on my tongue.

I raise my eyes and Blake is watching me. 'You are in bad trouble,' he says.

I don't take my finger out. 'What kind of trouble?' I mumble.

He smiles and is about to answer when a flash of surprised annoyance crosses his face. Its appearance and disappearance is swift. Very quickly his face resumes its neutral expression. I turn curiously to see what caused the disturbance. A silver-haired man is walking towards our table. When the man arrives, he totally ignores me, and looks only at Blake.

Blake's lips twist. 'Father, meet Lana. Lana, my father,' he introduces.

His father glances at me. His eyes are pale blue stones. He pushes his glasses up his nose. He looks quite mild and harmless. If I had seen him in the street, I would have smiled at him.

'Run along to the ladies and powder your nose or something. I need to speak to my son,' he says.

His impatience and rudeness is so unexpected it makes me gasp. I pick up my purse automatically and make to rise, but Blake's voice is like a whiplash. 'Stay,' he commands.

Surprised I meet his gaze. He is staring at me, his eyes forbidding and stern. I put my purse down, and he shifts his eyes from me to his father.

'When I have finished dinner I will come to you,' he says softly, and stands.

The old man says nothing. It is obvious that he is livid, but he turns around and leaves the restaurant.

Blake sits. 'Sorry about that,' he apologizes. 'My father can be brusque sometimes.'

'It's all right,' I say, but the incident has changed him. He has become remote and preoccupied.

He looks at my uneaten dessert. 'Do you want coffee?'

I shake my head and he calls for the bill. He puts me into a cab and watches as I am driven away.

Blake Law Barrington

After putting Lana into a cab I hail another and tell the driver to head to Claridges. I check my phone: my brother has called. I call him back.

'What's up, Marcus?'

'Have you seen Dad?'

'On my way to him now.'

'Any idea why he suddenly decided he must see you?'

'Nope,' I lie. We chat a bit more and then he hangs up.

I don't immediately to go up to my father's rooms. I stroll into the bar and order myself a large whiskey. A girl comes up to me.

'Hi,' she says. She is very expensively dressed and very seductive. A call girl. I can tell a mile off. 'Want to buy me a drink?'

I sigh and raise my hand. Instantly, the bartender comes to my side. I move my thumb in her direction. 'Get her a drink too,' I say.

The girl smiles at me. Ah, the clothes were bait, the hook is her smile. She is very beautiful. She has long, shining blonde hair that I can see is natural and pearly teeth. I so want to be distracted.

'You must be very rich and powerful,' she says.

'Why do you say that?'

'The way the bartender left what he was doing to serve you first. It's always a good sign of big money.'

'Where are you from?'

'Russia.' I nod and almost smile. Cliché of clichés. Of course, she is Russian.

'And you? You are American?'

'Yeah.'

'You are a very beautiful man. I'd really like to spend the night with you.'

I have never paid for sex. And then it hits me suddenly. I am paying for sex! It makes me laugh out loud.

'What is so funny?' the Russian asks.

'Why did you become a hooker?'

Her eyebrows arch. She is pure sophistication. 'Because I like nice things.' Then she deepens her voice until it is like hot caramel. She is very good at this. 'And I love a hot fuck with good-looking strangers.' She eyes my crotch greedily. She does it well and if I didn't know better I would think she was desperate for my body and not the contents of my wallet.

Lana's white face when my father ordered her to leave the table flashes into my mind. I down my drink and signal to the barman.

'Charge everything to my father's room,' I say, and leave a fifty-pound tip. My father is tight and actually goes through his hotel bills.

'Enjoy your drink,' I say to the Russian beauty, and make my way to the lift.

Upstairs, my father is waiting for me. As I expected the meeting does not go well.

'Do you think you are the first Barrington to be tempted?' my father asks me coldly.

'Tempted?'

'Tempted to throw it all away for a bit of flesh.'

'I don't want to throw it all away.'

'Really?'

'It honestly hasn't crossed my mind.'

'Do you think I am a fool? Do you think I cannot see what she is to you? Each one of us has a personal siren summoned from some demonic place, who enters our lives in the most mundane way, leads us to the very edge, and sings as we fall to our destruction. I had mine. Many years ago.'

I stare at him. A memory struggles to surface. A voice in my head, 'Don't go there, boy.' So I do not. Instead, I turn almost gratefully to my father's story. Even the thought of my father being in love is foreign, impossible.

He smiles frostily, his voice is calm and unemotional, but the memories must have been bitter for his mouth is a tightly controlled slash in his face. 'She was a redhead, a fledgling star. Every time I saw her, I could have ruined everything for her, but I fought it with every ounce of my being.'

'Where is she now?'

'Dead.'

'What happened?'

'It got so bad your grandfather paid a man to run off with her. She became a drug addict and died in a motel room. I saw the pictures and even then I felt an indescribable loss. But now, when I think back, I realize that my father was right. She was the enemy carefully chosen for me by fate. A beautiful butterfly. After she had destroyed me, after I'd lost everything, she would have carelessly moved on to the next flower.' He looks intently at me. 'What would happen if I paid your girl to leave you?'

Despite myself, I flush with anger. I turn away from him and start walking towards the door. 'I'll thank you to stay out of my business. I don't want to leave everything for her. It is only a fling. A temporary thing.'

I am so angry at my father's suggestion to pay Lana off that I walk the streets of London for almost an hour feeling strangely confused and lost. The only thing I know for sure is that I ache for her. With every fiber of my being, I ache for her.

I tell myself it is just lust. But I know, I know it isn't. It isn't lust when you want to reach out and wipe away her tears and press her body against your own. I don't just want to fuck her, I want to hold her after that. She fills the void inside me that has never been filled by the best schools, the most beautiful women, the fastest cars, the most expensive champagnes, or the most glamorous parties.

I take a cab back to St John's Wood and let myself in quietly. For a moment I stand at the mouth of the corridor. The living room is dim. Then I walk towards it —my feet soundless on the thick carpet—and stop at the threshold. Only the lampshade by the sofa is lit.

She has fallen asleep on the couch. Her fingers are slack and trailing down. There is an empty glass that has rolled away from her. I go to her and gaze down at her sleeping form. She is unbearably, impossibly beautiful. I put my hand under her neck and the other under her knees and lift her up. She moans softly, and I smell the alcohol on her breath.

'Don't leave me,' she mumbles.

I freeze. For a time I am completely still, but she does not awaken so I carry her to our bed and put her down. I bend down and kiss her soft lips. She is half-asleep, but she opens her mouth and I deepen the kiss. Her hands come up to my hair, her fingers entwine in the silky strands. She moans and arches her body towards me. I support her body with my forearms, and lifting her towards me begin to suck at her exposed throat.

'Please, Blake…' she gasps and molds her body into mine.

I let my mouth trail lower. At the soft swelling where her breast begins I stop and suck again. This time longer. I will leave my mark on her. She groans with pleasure. I take my mouth away and look at the red mark possessively. I feel like an adolescent again. She is mine. Mine to mark. I put my mouth on another part of her creamy skin and suck diligently.

Her hands are moving towards my belt. They are urgent but useless against the metal buckle. She is more than half drunk. I put my hand into her pajama trousers, slip it under her panties, and touch her between her legs. Her sex is wet and tingling for me. She has never begged me to enter her before. I want her to. I rip open her pajama top. A button hits the mirror in the room and makes a sound. She does not hear it.

I grab the ends of her trouser legs and tug. They slide off her and I fling them behind me. I tear at her panties. Then I latch my mouth on her nipple. Her head falls back and she sighs with abandonment. I gaze at the body exposed to me, mine to do with as I please. I have never felt the need to sexually possess anyone like this before. But she I must. She is like a craving. An addiction.

'Tell me you're mine,' I order hoarsely.

'I'm yours,' she says.

'Beg me to enter you,'

She obeys instantly. 'Please Blake, enter me. I want you to. Badly.'

'Open your legs and show me your pussy.'

She opens her legs and I see how wet and glistening her open flesh is.

I take off my shirt and my trousers while she watches from the bed. Her eyes are huge and strange with desire. I have never seen her like this. I want this woman so bad it feels like a forest fire is raging in my dick. I stand a moment longer savoring the way I feel. Hard, ready and so horny. That feeling of animal passion. This is my mate.

I own her.

I climb on the bed—the mattress gives under my weight—and enter her sweet flesh. She cries out, and then she is gripping me so hard, her nails dig into my flesh. I let her climax before I allow myself to. She falls asleep almost instantly and I lay my palm, the fingers spread out to full on her stomach. I recognize the possessiveness of the gesture. I turn to look at her sleeping face.

An image of my father flashes into my head. What the fuck am I doing? This is my fuck doll. Not my mate. Victoria smiles in my head. I cannot ruin my father's plan. They are also my plans. Soon. Soon I will tire of driving my dick deep into her sweet pussy.

Some deep part of me knows it is a lie, but I go to sleep snuggled against her warm, soft body, pretending to feel good. There is still time. Plenty of time to sort it all out.

Twenty four

Blake has a business dinner that he expects to run late, so Billie and I are going to a wine bar that has just opened in Seymour Place. I wash my hair and dress in a pair of tight jeans and the top that Fleur had called basic even though it is rather grand. It has lace and pearl buttons down the front. Tom is on holiday and Blake has left strict instructions for me to take a taxi to and fro. I go to visit my mother first.

The pouch with her supply of antineoplastons is strapped around her waist, but she looks well. She is steadily gaining weight, there is color again in her cheeks, and she seems in good spirits.

'My, don't you look nice,' she says, bustling me into the kitchen. She puts a skillet on the stove. 'You can't drink on an empty stomach. We are having grilled chicken and salad.'

She sprinkles nuts on a bowl of salad.

We sit to eat and it is like old times. Afterwards, she refuses all offers of help with the dishes and shoos me away. 'Go. Go and have a good time, you. Call me in the morning.'

'OK, OK,' I say laughing as I am bodily pushed out of her door.

At Billie's, I am ordered to lose the lace top and slip into one of Billie's skinny tops. I have to admit the red top looks hip and a whole lot sexier.

The taxi drops us outside the entrance of Fellini's. We open the wooden door and enter the dimly-lit interior. It is all green walls, chrome fittings and framed black and white photos of movie stars from the forties and fifties. The clientele is quite a mixed bag, but seems to be mostly office folk.

We find a table and I buy the first round. When it is Billie's turn, she goes up to the bar, and a guy sidles up to the half-circle seat that I am sitting on. He is wearing a suit and must be in his mid or late twenties. He smiles at me. Friendly face. I will also remember later that he looked clean and trustworthy. There is nothing about him to suggest otherwise

'Hello, doll,' he says. 'Can I buy you a drink?'

'Thanks, but my friend's gone to get me one.'

'Mind if I join you girls?'

'As a matter of fact, yes,' interrupts Billie rudely. She is standing behind me and actually glowering at the man. She looks quite tough and fierce.

'No problem,' he says immediately, and with a wink to me, gets up and goes back to join his friends, who are gathered at the bar. He says something to them and they slap him on the back and laugh uproariously. For some reason, their laughter disturbs me and makes me think it is somehow connected to me. But Billie is saying something and I turn my head to listen.

Blake Law Barrington

I feel my phone vibrate in my pocket and instantly perceive that it is from Lana. Why, I cannot say, for she has never called me before. I take my phone out of my pocket and look at the screen. Her number flashes. I excuse myself, walk away from the table, and lay my phone to my ear.

'Hi,' says a voice I do not recognize.

'Yes,' I reply, my voice is strangely abrupt. Some part of my brain registers surprise at the state of my voice.

'This is Billie, Lana's friend. Don't panic, but some wanker has slipped a roach into her drink, and she's gone down.'

Her accent is hard for me to understand, and I have never heard the term roach, but I guess instantly that Billie must be referring to a date rape drug. 'Gone down?' I repeat.

'Look, I've had to leave her at the table with one of the bar staff to come outside and call you, so could you hurry here, please?'

'Where are you?'

She gives me the address.

Without going back to the table to make my apologies, I rush out of the restaurant and drive like a mad man through speed cameras. I double park outside the entrance of Loren, and bound into the crowded bar. I stand at the entrance and let my eyes scan the room. A young girl with extremely white hair is waving at me.

Lana is slumped against her and her head is lolling on the girl's left shoulder.

As soon as I reach them she stands up and tries to keep Lana up with her hand, but Lana flops over it.

'It's not as bad as it looks,' Billie says. 'Almost all my friends have had it slipped into their drink before, and we've all survived.' She jerks her eyes towards a group of men. 'I think it's them over there, but over my dead body will they be taking this girl home with them.'

I glance over at the men. Six lads. Youngish. Their idea of fun. As soon as they sense my eyes on them, they quickly turn away and I experience a fury that I have never known. The urge to go over and punch their smirking faces burns my guts. I turn towards them, raging uncontrollably. A hand on my arm stops me. I look at it. The nails are painted to look like slices of watermelon. The sight has a strange effect on me. I lose the edge of my anger.

I drag my eye upwards.

'If you prop her up on one side, we can walk her out,' she urges. Her voice is surprisingly strong and purposeful. I had dismissed her, the spiders and the boiled-egg white hair, but she is more. No wonder Lana held her in such high regard.

'No need,' I say, and scoop Lana up easily.

'Oh!' Billie exclaims. Turning around she aggressively flicks her middle finger at the group of guys who have turned to watch, and follows me out of the restaurant. Outside, Billie opens the passenger door and I deposit Lana into the seat. I close the door and turn to face her.

'Thank you for calling me.'

She shrugs. 'No problem. Thanks for coming. Couldn't take her home. Her mum…you know how it is?'

I nod. 'How will you get home?'

'Oh, don't worry about me. I'll just hop on a bus.'

That makes me frown. 'Is that safe at this time of the night?'

Her eyes widen. Suddenly she seems so much younger. 'It's only ten o'clock, Mr. Barrington.'

I take my wallet out of my pocket, pull two fifties out, and hold them out to her. 'Here, take a cab.'

'Uh…taxis don't cost that much, Mr. Barrington.'

'Call me Blake, and please, don't argue with me,' I say impatiently.

She reaches out and takes the money, then shifts from one foot to another. 'It's not as bad as it looks. Tomorrow will be the killer. She'll think she's dying, but she'll be OK. Give her lots of water to drink.'

'Thanks again.'

'Oh, and if you want to do anything kinky to her now's the time. She won't remember a thing in the morning.'

For a moment I stare at her shocked, and then I realize that it is her attempt at a joke. I shake my head. Strange girl. She pulls Lana's phone out of her pocket. 'Here's her phone. She'll need to call her mum before twelve or there'll be trouble.'

I take it distractedly. 'OK, I'll make sure she does.' I walk over to the driver's side of the car and get in.

Billie Black

I watch his car roar powerfully into life, pick up great speed almost immediately, and take the corner at an alarming speed. Then I stuff the money into the back pocket of my black jeans and casually amble over to the bus stop. At the bus stop I sit on a cold plastic chair and replay the moment when Blake picked Lana up.

I will never have that, but instead of that usual tinge of envy because someone else has more than me, my little heart is soaring for Lana.

Yay! Banker boy cared.

Blake Law Barrington

Lana moans and I take my eyes off the road to briefly look at her.

'Ooh uuugggg why uuuuuuggggg,' she says, and covering her face with her hand, mumbles unintelligently. I don't try to talk to her. When I reach the apartment block, I take my keycard from the dashboard and go out to Lana's side. The night porter's eyes are round with curiosity when I carry Lana through reception towards the lift. He stands up, but I shake my head, and he sits down again. I elbow the lift button and it opens almost immediately. I slot in my card and we are transported upwards. The movement of the elevator makes Lana stir in my arms.

'Sorry, Mummy,' she says. 'Oh it's you'… more gibberish…then clearly, 'where's Mum?'

'She's home safe.'

But she appears not to hear, and seems to be trapped in some nightmare of her own. 'Don't die, Mummy. You promised to come to my wedding.'

I watch her with a frown.

'You said you would.' She begins to cry. 'Mum, it's cold. I'm so cold.'

I curse. The lift door opens and I carry her into the apartment and deposit her on the bed.

She grasps my arm and looks into my eyes, frowns, and does not seem to recognize me. 'Where's my mother?' She shivers.

I cover her. 'Shhh…'

'I'll tell you now. You won't break me, Barrington,' she slurs and turns on her side. 'I'll tell Jack what you did. He'll sort you out. Jaaaacccckk,' she wails.

It makes the hair on my neck stand to see her this way, but it is only when she starts talking gobbledygook in earnest that I get worried. I go into the kitchen and phone my doctor.

After a few minutes I end the call and stare at the granite top. I am simmering with anger—with her, for being so careless, so naïve, and with those pigs that thought they could drug a girl and rape her. My hands clench. I close my eyes and breathe deeply. They didn't get her. They didn't get her. My hands unclench. I take another full breath. It is not her fault. She is as innocent as a child. Grimly, I go to sit by the bedside and listen to her ramblings. In all of them, I am the enemy. The one who wants to use her for sex.

I clasp my hands tightly and remain silent.

The porter brings the doctor up. Dr. Faulks is very quick with his analysis. There is nothing much to do. Wait it out. Fluids are the key. Tomorrow will be bad. She will have memory lapses, most likely won't remember a thing.

'Oh, plastic sheets might be a good idea. Sometime incontinence can occur.'

After the doctor is gone, I undress her.

She sighs elaborately. 'Oh! It's you again.' She seems confused, sad.

I pull the duvet over her and she pushes it away. 'I'm hot. Really hot. I thought you wanted to fuck me, anyway.' She grabs my hand and kisses it. 'Thank you. Thank you for what you did for my mother.' Then she moans and falls into a stupor. She sleeps for half an hour and wakes up retching. I bring a large salad bowl that I find in the kitchen, but it is only dry heaving.

I lay a cold towel on her forehead. Her fingers come up to push it away. She pulls my face towards her. Her breath smells strange and stale, but I don't care, I kiss her back.

Suddenly she turns away and begins to cry.

For hours I sit beside her as she goes from comatose to babbling idiot to crazed sex fiend, all the time wondering when it will be over. Finally, when the sky is beginning to lighten, purely from exhaustion she falls into a restless sleep.

I text Laura to reschedule my morning appointments and get into bed beside her. I put my arm around her narrow waist and close my eyes with relief that her suffering is over for the night, and hope that she won't remember this long and terrible night. My nose hovers over the crook of her neck and finds the faint but familiar scent of her perfume.

I register in my tense body a sense of victory that they did not get her, and then, a strong sense of possession. I tighten my hold on her.

She belongs to me until I say otherwise.

Twenty five

Lana Bloom

While we are having dinner on the balcony I say, 'We've been invited to a party tomorrow. Do you want to go?'

Blake looks at me strangely. 'It's my birthday tomorrow.'

'Oh,' I exclaim, surprised. 'You never said anything.'

'No, it's not something I am looking forward to.'

'You will be thirty.'

'Yes.'

'Do you want to come to the party then?'

'I can't. My family is flying over to be with me. They've arranged something for me in a hotel. It will be insufferably boring, I'm sure, but I am obliged to attend.'

"Of course, of course.' I try my best not to show how his news has affected me. Was he never going to tell me? 'I'll just go to the party with Billie, then.'

Only this morning I tasted the name Lana Barrington on my tongue. The whisper is my secret. It felt right. Or as Billie would say, very fucking right. So I said it louder.

'Lana Barrington.' Daring the fates.

Mrs. Lana Barrington. Your husband has been delayed. Would you like to wait for him at the bar?

The fantasy was so perfect I wanted to cry. What a fool I have been. How on earth did I manage to fall in love with such a cold and heartless man, a banker for God's sake?

'Let Tom drive you there and back,' he is saying.

'It's OK. I'll just take a taxi.'

"I'll feel better if Tom drives you, waits for you and brings you back.'

'Will she be there?'

'Yes,' he says very quietly.

'Well, that's that then. I hope you have fun.' My voice sounds high and too merry.

'I won't,' he says, but that doesn't soothe me one bit.

That was yesterday. Today I am in Billie's bedroom wearing a pair of white shorts, a cut off, sleeveless, white T-shirt that leaves my midriff bare and white trainers.

‘Wow, you look seriously hot,’ Billie comments.

‘You don’t think it’s too slutty?’

‘Are you kidding? It’s white. You look like a wet dream. Besides, it’s Jerry’s party. It’s always full of working girls.’

Billie is wearing combat boots, a fur trimmed, green beret, and a clinging black cat-suit.

‘Well, you look very Miley Cyrus,’ I say.

‘Thanks. I was going for rock chick, but obviously I’m not ever going to say no to Miley,’ Billie replies with a grin. ‘Now get in front of the mirror.’

I sit on the edge of the bed and Billie picks up a curling iron and takes up position behind me. With meticulous care she begins to put corkscrew curls in my hair. She is concentrating so hard she does not speak, so I let my mind wander to Blake. I wonder about his world. So entirely different from mine. At a hotel, he said, careful not to mention the name of the hotel, as if he feared there was a possibility that I might turn up and embarrass him.

In a little while Leticia comes to join us. She is wearing a plain gray T-shirt, ripped jeans and a surly expression. Her hair is gelled to spikes around her head. She is a big, butch girl.

‘How’s it going, Let?’ I greet.

Leticia grunts moodily.

Suddenly, an image of Leticia tied spread eagle on her bed with a chocolate bar stuck between her legs pops into my head and I press my lips together to hide my amusement.

Leticia turns towards Billie. ‘You told her, didn’t you?’ she accuses.

Unfazed, Billie takes another small section of my hair and carefully coils it around the curling iron. ‘Be thankful I didn’t tell her what I did to you last night,’ she says, and crusty, cross Leticia squirms.

When we are ready, we walk over to Jerry's place. It is such a warm evening we don't even need coats.

The music is loud and there are many people there, but Billie, who is always the centre of any party, gets immediately pulled to the middle of the dance floor. When my mobile rings I almost do not hear it. I look at the screen. It is ten o'clock and it is Blake.

'Hi,' I say, but it is so loud it's impossible to hear him. 'Wait one moment,' I yell and fight my way out of the crowd. 'What's up?'

'Nothing. My party was rather flat, so I left. Can I come join you, after all?'

'Of course.' Suddenly my heart feels light and happy. He wants my company.

I am sitting on the stairs waiting for him when he arrives.

'Where's Tom?'

'Sent him home.'

He locks his car and walks up to me. 'What are you doing sitting here?'

'Waiting for you.'

He turns to look at a group of youths. They are swearing loudly and holding beer cans. 'It looks dangerous.'

I laugh. 'I grew up here. I know those guys. They're Jerry's mates. If you want to score some coke, they're the ones to go to.'

'You don't take drugs, do you?'

I laugh again. 'No.'

He sits beside me, and takes a curly lock of hair in his hand. 'What's this?'

'Billie did it. It's not permanent.'

His hands move to the white shorts. 'And this?'

'I can hardly wear the fancy dresses you bought me here. I'll stick out like a sore thumb.' I look at him hungrily: the man looks good enough to eat. A soft breeze teases his hair. I have a desire to flirt with him. 'Don't you like it, then?'

He looks at me expressionlessly, a master of disguise. 'What do you think?'

'I think yes.'

'Go to the top of the class, Miss Bloom.'

I laugh.

He watches me closely. 'I don't think I have ever seen you laugh.'

'And?'

'I like it.'

I giggle. 'Good. Let's go find you a drink.'

'Is my car safe there?'

'It's not Detroit, you know.'

He jerks his head at the group of youths with the beer cans. 'Are you sure?'

I look around and further away notice Kensington standing with a group of boys watching us. I point my thumb over my shoulder. 'See that boy in the green baseball cap? If you give him a ride he'll watch your car for you.'

Blake looks over at the boy.

'That black boy?' he says doubtfully.

'Be careful, you might reveal your hand as not being an equal opportunities employer.'

Blake crooks a finger in the boy's direction. Kensington doesn't need any further encouragement. He jumps on his bike and tucking his head into his shoulders races towards us. He screeches to a stop dangerously close to Blake's feet.

'Oi! Watch it,' I warn.

'Sorry,' he apologizes with a cheeky grin.

'What's your name?'

'Kensington Parish.'

'Want to watch my car for me, Kensington?'

'Yeah,' Kensington agrees enthusiastically. He looks at the car admiringly. 'This car was made by God, man.'

'Here's fifty.'

Kensington's eyes sparkle. 'Fifty quid?'

His thin hand reaches out for it, but Blake pulls his hand back slightly. 'If I come back and find the car exactly as I left it then there's another fifty for you.'

Kensington's face splits into an almighty grin. 'Thanks, Mister,' he says and snatches the note. Unceremoniously, he drops his bicycle on the ground and hops lightly onto the bonnet of the car.

'You're generous,' I say.

'Not at all. A single scratch can cost thousands to repair.'

We go up the stairs and find Billie. Billie makes a licking gesture behind his back, but she is very polite. 'Forget about good Scotch here,' she says, and goes to get Blake a beer. As we are talking, Jack walks in. He has a pretty girl on his arm and he introduces her as Alison.

'Hello, Alison. Great to meet you,' I say warmly, and turning to Jack, widen my eyes to say well done. He pretends he has not seen my gesture and, briefly shakes hands with Blake.

'Right, I want you lot on your feet and dancing,' Billie orders bossily, as she thrusts a bottle of beer into Blake's palm.

'I don't dance,' Blake says, as Jack and Alison quickly move off in the opposite direction.

A couple vacate one of the battered sofas. 'Perhaps you would like to join me on one of these lovely sofas,' Blake says, and collapses into its creaky springs. I laugh and fall next to him. A young man who looks the worse for wear comes and sits next to me on the sofa. He has a tattoo of men in a tug-of-war on his shaven head. Blake mutters something indecipherable and scoops me up and deposits me on his lap.

'What are you doing?' I squeal.

'Don't want you catching anything off him,' he whispers in my ear.

I feel the hard muscles of his thighs. Flirtatiously, I look at him from beneath my lashes. He puts his big hands on my bare knees and pulls me until my rear is in close contact with his groin. I can feel how hard he has become.

Blake pulls me closer and captures my mouth. He smells of caramel and tastes divine. I slip my hand into his unbuttoned shirt, and find a man's skin, hot, taut, muscles rippling underneath. It makes my lips part.

'I want to take you home now,' he growls in my ear.

'OK,' I agree instantly, and we stand to go.

'Leaving so soon,' Bill moans moodily.

'It's not really my scene,' Blake says.

'Call me tomorrow,' Jack says, as I kiss his cheek.

'I will.'

I turn to Alison, who is holding onto Jack possessively, as if she fears something is going on between Jack and me. 'Take care of my brother,' I whisper in her ear and see her relax and smile warmly for the first time.

Then Blake and I are leaving, holding hands, as if we are real lovers. As if he has not paid me to have sex with him. As if I am not the living, breathing doll that he expects to get bored with in a few weeks.

Outside, Kensington hops off the car bonnet when he spots us.

'Good job,' Blake says and slips him the other fifty.

'Cool. What about a ride, then?'

'Another time,' replies Blake, opening the passenger door for me.

Blake is very quiet in the car. Suddenly he reaches past me to the glove box and takes out a velvet box. He tosses it into my lap. 'I got you a present.'

'On *your* birthday?'

'I thought it would look great on you. Besides, what's the point of having a rich lover if you don't unearth expensive baubles out of him.'

I release the catch on the box. It opens and I gasp. On a bed of satin lies the most beautiful seven strand pearl necklace with a large oval sapphire centre.

'Oh my!' I say, staring at it.

At the next red light, he takes the necklace from my stunned hands and puts it around my throat while I hold my hair up. I feel his warm fingers on the back of my neck. Then the light changes and his fingers are gone. I turn around to face him, full of anticipation.

He takes his eyes off the road. 'Beautiful,' he says.

I look at myself in the visor mirror. Even in the dim light, the diamonds set around the large sapphire sparkle like stars. I didn't get him anything.

'I didn't get you anything.'

His eyes drift away from the road and rest on me briefly. 'I didn't expect anything from you.'

'Did you get lots of presents from your family?'

'We don't do presents. We already have everything we could want. When we were younger we did give each other joke gifts. But how many times can you give someone a blow-up doll or a penis enlargement gadget? It was a relief when that stopped.'

When we get to the apartment he picks me up in his arms, throws me on the bed and lunges in after me.

'This is a dangerously sexy pair of white shorts, Miss Bloom,' he teases. 'Do you have the necessary license to operate such a weapon?'

'It's not mine. It belongs to Billie,' I answer primly.

'Ah, Billie of the ear biting fame. Do you think she might let me buy it from her?'

'Oooo I don't know. It did come from a very exclusive market stall in Kilburn. There are only five hundred thousand others like it.'

His eyebrows rise, his lips curve. 'That rare?'

'That rare.'

'I better make my bid good then.'

'Good idea, Mr. Barrington. Kill the competition in one fell swoop.'

'As her agent, what do you suggest I offer?'

'I believe she is hankering after a pink car.'

His eyes gleam. 'Are you sure, Miss Bloom, that I am not better off approaching the market dealer directly?'

'Of course you can… But it will not have the Lana Bloom scent,' I say daringly.

His eyes widen and fill with delicious longing. 'You never said a truer word, Miss Bloom.'

His long fingers very deliberately pop the top button and pull down the zip. The sound is exciting in the silence. I can hear my own ragged breathing. He slides the shorts off.

'Ah, these legs… So long… So silky… I swear I never met a girl with skin such as yours.'

The shorts slip over my ankles and end up clutched in his big hands. He crushes them, brings them to his nose and inhales deeply. 'The Lana Bloom scent. I'll miss it,' he whispers, almost to himself.

And suddenly I tense. All this will end soon.

This apartment, this bed, these clothes, this delicious banter, this *man*…will all disappear into nothing. I will be left only with memories. I clutch his forearms, pull his mouth down to mine, and kiss him desperately, opening my mouth, begging him to be inside me. He has already left his mark on me. I must leave my mark on him. I lie under him naked but for my necklace, and realize I don't know how to.

When the desert wind blew it covered everything in sand.

Twenty six

'Remember when you said you wanted to be part of my world? Do you still want to?' he asks me.

'Yes.'

'It is very ugly.'

My answer is instant. 'I don't care. I want to know.'

For a moment, he hesitates, there is doubt there, and then an indescribable expression flashes in his eyes. 'All right. Let's go.' He leads me to a BMW parked up the street. I look at him questioningly.

'Hired,' he says briefly.

'Where are we going?'

'Somewhere in the New Forest.'

We drive in silence, the atmosphere in the car, taut and foreign, and come to a stop outside what seems to be a lodge of some kind. The building is small and unremarkable. There are other cars parked in the car park, but something feels off key.

'They are all hired, aren't they?'

'Yes,' he says shortly. 'Come.'

While I look around me, he gets out of the car, opens the boot and takes out two boxes. I look at my watch. 10.00p.m.

We go into the low building and enter a large empty room with many doors. All the doors are open except one. I shiver. Something about the place doesn't feel right. We enter one of the rooms and Blake closes the door behind us. There is nothing in that room except a table and a mirror. Blake puts the two boxes on the table.

'You wanted to come into my world. Here's your chance. Are you sure?'

He looks different. His eyes and voice are cold. He is hoping I will say no, but I want to enter his world. So badly, I throw caution to the wind. I lick my suddenly dry lips, swallow, and nod.

He holds out the box tied with a red ribbon and I take it from him. It is not heavy. 'What's in it?'

'Open it and see.'

He watches me untie the ribbon and lift the lid. I push aside the tissue and find a mask. White and pretty. I raise my eyes to his. 'Do I put it on?'

'Not yet.'

I put the mask aside and take out the bulky red garment inside. It is a cloak with a hood. I look at him, my expression begs the question, 'What? What is this all about?'

He ignores my unspoken query. 'Wear it.'

I slip into it and he steps forward and does the large button at my throat. The cloak is thick and voluminous and covers me entirely. Deftly, he pulls the hood up, and fits the mask on my face. He stands me in front of the mirror.

'Remember,' he warns. 'Do not take this ensemble off after we leave this room. No matter what happens the mask and the robes do not come off. Do you understand?'

My mask nods in the mirror.

He opens his box and dresses himself in the black robes that are inside. His mask is gold with a beaked nose. Unlike mine his seems sinister and forbidding.

'Ready?'

'Yes.'

He puts his hand in the small of my back and guides me out of the room. We cross the large empty space and go through another door. It turns out to be the back door of the lodge. A man sitting on a horse-drawn coach is waiting. He does not turn to look at us but stares straight ahead. The bizarre and forbidding alchemy of the moment causes me to blankly note the white socks on the horse. We climb in and the coachman immediately sets the horse to a trot. We follow a path that snakes through woods until we suddenly come upon a grand mansion perched on higher ground.

My breath is swept away by it. Made of cut gray stone, it is like something found in a windswept ghost story. Awestruck, I stare at the roaring gargoyles and the many soaring gothic spires that pierce the purple sky. Hundreds of windows stare out like glassy dead eyes. Unless I am very much mistaken one of the windows blinks, a flash of yellow iris, before it snaps shut. Someone was watching our arrival.

The coach comes to a stop on the entrance stairs and we climb out. I feel Blake's hand on my waist as he helps me out.

'Remember, the mask does not come off, even in the ladies.'

'OK.'

'And don't tell anyone your name.'

'OK.'

'Don't speak unless spoken to.'

'Right.'

'I'm serious, Lana.'

I look up into the eyeholes of his mask. 'You're making me nervous, Blake.'

'It's important.'

'Then don't leave my side.'

'I've no intention of doing that.'

We go up the shallow stone steps. When we reach the top, I turn to look down upon the magnificent garden maze. In the purplish light it is very beautiful. At the entrance, a totally expressionless, bone-thin man, dressed in black coat-tails, nods at Blake and slowly waves his hand towards the interior of the house.

There are more ushers and silent staff dressed in black who nod at us and wave us deeper into the interior. The funereal garments and the silence begin to seep into me. I recognize them to be poisonous.

Finally, two men open a pair of double doors and we enter a large hall full of masked, robed people standing around and talking in whispers. There is a stage at one end with a throne on it. The room reminds me of an old-fashioned theater with balconies. There are also many doors that lead away from the hall. A strange throbbing music is playing into that odd air of expectancy and waiting.

I look up at Blake. 'This reminds me of *Eyes Wide Shut*.'

'Yes, Stanley Kubrick's movies are filled with hidden messages.'

A waiter brings a tray. Blake shakes his head. When I try to reach for a glass, I feel the subtle pressure that he exerts on my hand. I shake my head and the waiter moves on silently. It is at this point that I realize that there are other women besides me who are wearing the exact same robe and mask as me.

'Hello,' a man's voice addresses us from behind.

We turn. A stocky man in an odd gray and silver mask is standing about a foot away from us. 'You brought…someone,' he says, his eyes glittering blackly through the eyeholes of his mask. I feel Blake tense beside me.

'Yes.'

'Will you be going into the main room?' the man asks.

'Of course,' Blake says smoothly, but I feel the tremor that goes through his body.

'Good, I will see you there. If I don't, tell your father I send my regards.'

Blake nods, and the man turns on his heel and disappears into the crowd of robes and masks.

'Come,' Blake says urgently, and leads me towards the entrance. The large doors open, and we retrace our steps out into the evening air. We go down the shallow steps and into a waiting coach.

When I turn to Blake, he puts a finger to his lips. The coach drops us off outside the lodge house, we traverse that strange empty room, and go back out to where the hired car is waiting. Blake unlocks the car.

'Take your cloak off and drop it on the ground,' he orders as he takes his own cloak off and chucks it into the back seat.

I do as I am told and get into the car. My hands are trembling. Blake's fear and tension have transferred themselves to me.

Blake starts the engine and the car screeches away. He says nothing and drives very fast.

'Chuck the mask out of the window,' he says when he has been driving for about five minutes. He takes his mask off and flips it onto the back seat where it lands on his black cloak.

'Why did I have to throw mine away but not you?'

'Yours is generic; my cloak has my family insignia sewn into it and my mask is distinct to me.'

Ten minutes later, Blake pulls off the road and, turning around, takes me into his arms. 'I'm sorry,' he says. 'I shouldn't have taken you there. I don't know what I was thinking of. You're just a baby.'

'It's OK,' I say, confused. 'Nothing happened.'

He looks into my eyes. He is full of secrets. 'Yes, nothing happened.'

That night he jerks awake in a cold sweat and sits upright. The movement wakes me.

'Did you have a nightmare?' I ask, my hand reaching for his back.

'I dreamed I took you into the main room,' he says. His voice is hoarse with horror.

'What happens in the main room?'

He turns to me and in the dark his eyes are tormented pools of terror. 'Oh, Lana, Lana, Lana,' he whispers in my hair.

'Tell me,' I urge, but he shakes his head.

'My world is ugly and corrupt. It only looks good from the outside. When our time is over, I must return you the way I found you, pure and innocent.'

Gently he opens my legs. 'Let me hide a little while longer in your world,' he rasps and buries his mouth in my sex.

His mouth is warm and soft. My body responds, arches; my hands come out to grasp his hair; my legs entwine like ropes around his head, and I come with a gasp while I am wonderfully full of him, but through it all I never forget what he said—*when our time is over.*

Twenty seven

I wake up and turn around to look at the man beside me. In the dim light I stare at him. He is so heartbreakingly beautiful when he sleeps he makes me want to cry. That hard mouth softened, the thick, stubby eyelashes dark-blue smudges on his face. I slip out of bed quietly. I am ravenous these days. I smile to think it must be all the sex. I close the bedroom door softly and pad into the kitchen where I switch on the light and head towards the fridge. My hands reach for the tin of caviar and a jar of marmalade. I go to the breadbox and cut two slices of nutty bread. Those I pop into the toaster and stand by the counter, yawning.

When they are ready, I spread a thick layer of caviar on one slice of toast and spoon a dollop of marmalade over the other. I slap them together, and popping myself on a stool, bite into my creation. It is so delicious I close my eyes to savor it. I open my mouth eagerly to take a second bite.

'Is this another terrible combination that you Brits have conjured up?' Blake teases from the doorway.

My eyes snap open, my mouth closes, and my eyes move over the food I have prepared. Marmalade and caviar. Slowly my gaze lifts to him. He is lounging against the doorframe nude as the day he was born.

'What's the matter?' he asks.

I close my mouth and try to smile. 'It's my own thing,' I say weakly. My heart is beating so loud in my ears that I feel as if he must be able to hear it. I put the sandwich down and look at him. 'Can't you sleep?'

'Come back to bed and put me to sleep,' he invites, his eyes darkening.

'OK, I'll finish my sandwich and come join you. Go ahead.'

I smile at him, willing him not to enter the kitchen, but go back to the bedroom and wait for me. He looks at me and as if he has heard my unspoken wishes he nods and, turning around, leaves. The air escapes my lungs in a rush. I put my elbow on the surface of the counter and lean my forehead against my hand. I actually feel sick. I open the sandwich and really look at what I have concocted. At the smeared caviar and marmalade. It is revolting.

My mother ate anchovies and marmalade when she was pregnant.

I cover my mouth.

I am pregnant.

I look at the clock above the door. It is two in the morning. I close the sandwich, my appetite totally gone. Oh God, what now? I begin to count backwards.

Yes, I am definitely two weeks late.

Twenty eight

Blake Law Barrington

I open the door to the apartment and instantly *feel* that she is gone. Not gone out shopping or gone to see her mother, but gone away from me. Forever. Her presence seems to have evaporated into thin air. I push down the sensation of horror and walk down the corridor to the living room.

The curtains are drawn shut. It is dim and cool. I move to the coffee table. It is empty. In the bedroom, I glance towards my bedside table then hers. Nothing. I go into the kitchen and look at the island top, my eyes scanning the room quickly.

No, she has left no note.

I go back into the bedroom and open the cupboard. Handbags, shoes, clothes. It is all there. She has taken nothing. I key in the combination and open the safe. The velvet box is in there. I open it and the necklace lays nestled on its satin bed. I sigh with relief, put it back and close the safe.

On my way to the living room I pass the dining room, my eyes skim the long table and fall on her purse. For an odd moment, I find myself staring at it. The thoughts in my brain are foreign. I shake my head and walk away. Three steps down the corridor, I stop and go back. Like a sleepwalker I drift to her bag. I put a hand out and lift it by its strap, a metal and black leather interlaced affair.

I raise the flap and look inside.

Lip gloss, ballpoint pen, compact mirror, sparkly eye shadow and…a small maroon wallet. I fish it out, run my finger along the leather and open it. I look at what appears to be a collage of photographs cut out from different photographs and carefully, lovingly stuck together: her mother, Billie and Jack. The child-like innocence of her handiwork causes me pain.

I do not know why it should. I close the flap, return the wallet to her handbag, and walk away from the dining room. I have never done such a thing before. My shoulders feel tense with worry and confusion. What is the matter with me? I have never been curious about the contents of any other woman's purse before.

She must have gone to visit her mother.

I ring her number and wait, but on the second ring I hear another ring coming from the living room. I follow the sound; her phone is lying on the sofa. I cut the connection and pick up her phone.

Last caller, me, last call, her mother.

I ring her mother's landline. It rings out. I go through her address list and ring Billie. When her cocky recorded voice comes on I leave a message for her to call me back urgently. Then I ring Jack. He answers on the sixth ring just as I am about to give up.

'Jack, do you know where Lana is?'

'No, why?'

'Just trying to find her. She's gone out without her cellphone.'

'It's raining here. Is it raining there?'

The question throws me and there is a slight pause before I reply. 'Yeah… It's raining here.'

'I wouldn't worry, mate, she's probably just gone out walking in the rain.'

'Right.'

Jack laughs. 'She'll come home looking like a drowned kitten. It's something to behold.'

'Right. Thanks, Jack.'

I go out onto the balcony. It is pouring with rain. A jagged flash of lightning splits the sky and I wait for the thunder. It comes deafeningly loud almost immediately. I frown. I don't like the thought of her in the rain. I go to the edge of the balcony and reach a hand out to catch some rain. Strange. I lean over the edge and turn my face up to the shower. I have not felt rain on my face since I was a child.

I try to imagine what she must be feeling, thinking. The rain is cold and I am quickly drenched. I peel off my shirt and as I am balling it in my hand I hear the key in the door. It opens and we stare at each other. Both wet. Both lost.

Instantly I know she is not the same anymore. There is such hurt in her eyes. I stride toward her. She is almost blue with cold.

'Come,' I say quickly, and taking her to the bathroom, guide her shivering body under the shower spray.

The water that pelts my cold skin is perfectly hot. I hear him moving away and I close my eyes and savor the pleasant sensation. Almost immediately I feel life and warmth coming back into my fingers and limbs. I have walked too long. I lean my forearms against the tiles and lifting my face to the water, abandon myself to it. I hear the shower door slide and my eyes open to him.

He is nude and standing outside.

My eyes rove over him and settle in fascination on his manhood that is already half erect before I suddenly realize what I am doing, and flushing with embarrassment, turn away.

He catches me by the chin and brings my eyes to him. 'I want you to look at me. Look at me.'

I return my eyes to his growing shaft. It is no longer at half-mast but standing proud. I lift my eyes back to his face and he steps into the shower. I move back to make space for him and watch him through the drops of water and steam. He chuckles and, finding the soap, slips it across the skin of my chest.

'Lift your arms.'

I obey and he soaps me under my arms. His touch is light and unticklish. He swipes the soap along my shoulders and then down to my breasts. Here he is rhythmic and meticulous. The mounds get much attention. So much that I long to have him take my nipples in his mouth.

The soap travels downward. To my stomach and lower still to my bare-skinned sex. He doesn't have to ask. Willingly, I spread my legs and the soap slides between them. The water sluices through his hands.

'Turn around.'

I turn. The soap slides sensuously along my back and down my spine to my hips and finally enters the crack of my bottom. I feel him kneel to wash my legs down to the soles of my feet, which he lifts and does one by one. Then he stands. In my line of sight I see him return the soap and pick up the shampoo bottle. I hear it squirt into the palm of his hand.

Then he is washing my hair.

The bubbles run down my body and heat collects between my legs.

He moves closer until I can feel his hard body slipping and sliding against mine. My legs begin to tremble. He turns me around and sucks my nipples while his hands slide down my stomach and boldly without warning grab my hips.

I gaze into the storm clouds in his eyes. His jaw is clenched tight. He lifts my body and penetrates me. I curl my legs around his hips and cry with animalistic pleasure. The deeper he buries himself inside me, the more my body cleaves to his.

Afterwards he carries me to the bed and dries me carefully.

I look up to him. 'What are you thinking of?'

'Your body.'

'Hmm.'

'Why did you walk so far in the rain?'

I stare into his eyes. They are unreadable. 'I like the rain. I've always walked in the rain.'

'But the rain in England is cold.'

'I don't know any other type of rain.'

He brings the hairdryer and a brush and sits on the bed with them beside him. Then he calls me to sit on the floor against the bed between his knees and begins to towel dry my hair. He is careful not to rub hard. Afterwards, he runs his fingers through my hair and gently untangles any knots he finds. Only then does he switch on the hairdryer and begin to dry my hair.

When he switches off the hairdryer I say, 'You can't cook but you can blow dry hair.'

'I used to dry my sister's hair for her.'

I swivel my neck around. 'You don't have a sister.'

Firmly he turns my head to face away from him. 'I've told you before, don't trust everything Wikipedia says.'

The brush glides through my hair in long, slow strokes. 'Why is she not known to the public?'

'She was born with a genetic anomaly. She's not like you and me. She lives in her own world. Most great families have such relatives—they just don't acknowledge or advertise them. It's an unfortunate effect of interbreeding.'

'So she is locked away?'

There is a pause. 'Something like that.'

'Do you still see her?'

'No, she is in our Buckinghamshire property. She has a whole wing and sectioned off grounds. Nurses and servants to care for her twenty-four hours a day.'

'What's she like?'

'A four-year-old child. She communicates by pointing and smiling.' His voice is sad.

'Why did you stop going to see her?'

The brush stops for a second, then starts again. 'The last time I saw her was when I was twelve. I was brushing her hair and my mother walked into the room. She was horrified. "Are you going to become a great man like your father or a sissy like your great uncle George?" He is another family member that we all pretend doesn't exist. I never went back after that.'

I turn around and catch his wrist. 'I don't care what anybody else says, you are a good man,' I say.

'Don't fool yourself, Lana. We're all no good. Don't trust any of us. Not even me.'

'Is there no one you trust?'

'No.'

'Not even your dad?'

'Dad?' he repeats sarcastically. 'My father's a sociopath.'

'Isn't he a great philanthropist?'

'Naïve little Lana. My father's a trillionaire. And there is no such thing as a philanthropist trillionaire. Do you know what one has to do to become a philanthropist trillionaire? Spend your whole life crushing as many people as possible for profit and then donate a library? I don't trust him and neither should you. It would cause him the same grief to obliterate you if you stood in his way as it would if he trod on an ant in his path.'

'Do trillionaires exist?'

The brush stills mid-air. 'Think, Lana. What is the debt of the United States alone? Who are all those lovely trillions owed to?'

'The Federal Reserve?'

He laughs. 'And who do you think owns that? The Federal Reserve is a private company just like the Bank of England, and every central bank throughout the world. Through a network of holding companies, the old families own vast controlling portions of not only their stocks, but all the too-big-to-fail banks that you hate so much.'

I frown. I need time to think about the true meaning of what he has revealed to me. 'What about your mother?'

'My mother threw us to the wolves a long time ago. My brothers and I grew up in stifling conditions.'

I shake my head. 'And there I was, wishing I was rich, while I was growing up in stifling conditions.'

'You don't understand, Lana, and perhaps you never will. We are different. We are not merely rich. We don't own tracts of land, we own countries and politicians. We have different responsibilities. We have an agenda.'

Then his face closes over.

Twenty nine

Blake Law Barrington

Your hands are inside my heart.

I stand on the embankment watching the water rushing by and think of Lana… and feel confused. There is a room inside her that I cannot enter. It is like the room inside me that she is not allowed in. It is where she keeps all the hurts I have caused. There are other things in that room, too. She has secrets now. I try to imagine what else could be hidden there.

A man talking loudly on his cell phone in some European language intrudes on my musings. I glance away from the water and see the tramps sleeping rough. For the first time in my life I perceive them as people. People who have fallen on hard times because of the things that *my* family is doing. They are not the real parasites. Lana was right that night when she accused us of being the real parasites. Of course, I have always known that we are the disease that they are ill from. You have to be blind, deaf and dumb not to see that. I just never cared before.

My phone rings. It is Marcus.

'Hello Marcus.'

My brother gets to the point immediately. 'Morgan just called me. *Why* is his loan still pending?'

'Morgan is a crook.'

There is a shocked silence and then my brother sighs heavily. 'What's going on with you, Blake?'

'Nothing. It bugs me to approve the loan. This green energy thing is such a scam.'

'Of course it is. And so what?'

'Why do we have to be part of everything crooked?'

'My God, you're beginning to sound like Quinn,' my brother says referring to our youngest sibling. Quinn turned his back on the family fortune and ran off to Europe to be an artist.'

'I'm beginning to think Quinn had the right idea.'

'It's a big account—government approved. We're just facilitating the funds.'

'We're always only facilitating the funds.'

'Father worked hard to get us on board. The other banks will kill for an opportunity like this.'

I sigh heavily. 'Yeah, I'll sign off on the papers in the morning.'

'I don't care about the loan—what I care about is what's happening to you? You're still in training. You can't get soft, Blake. These are shark-infested waters you're swimming in. They'll eat you alive. The entire system is corrupt. You can't fight it. If you try to, it will only break you.'

'Just having a bad day, I guess.'

'Have you spoken to Victoria?'

I frown. 'No, why?'

'Nothing. Her father was telling me you haven't called in some weeks. It's not a good thing to leave these things for too long.'

I do something I have never done before. I confide in my brother. 'I think I might have found someone.'

There is a shocked pause. 'Someone? What do you mean someone?'

'I think I'm in love.'

'What?' The burst of sound is so explosive and sudden that I have to pull the phone away from my ear and hold it away.

'Hell! Blake! Have you lost your mind?'

'I don't think so.'

'Who is it?'

'Not one of us.'

'Set her up in an apartment and visit her every day until you are bored of her.'

I smile in the dark. 'Done that.'

'You've fallen for a gold-digger!'

'She's not a gold-digger.'

'They all are.'

'Well, she's not.'

'Look, Blake, don't fuck this up. This is your future. You have to marry Victoria.'

'I don't have to do anything. I don't want to end up like you. A wife you detest, three kids you never see, and cold fucks with models and movie stars in luxurious apartments and hotel rooms.'

'What's wrong with that?'

It was a mistake to tell him.

'You're going to fuck this up, aren't you? This is not a club, Blake. You can't terminate your membership and walk away. There are consequences.'

'Quinn did.'

'You're *not* Quinn,' he says, his voice heavy with meaning.

'Look, I got to go. I'll call you soon. Bye, Marcus.'

I cut the call and stand looking at the cold, black water.

'Spare some change, mate,' someone says from behind.

I turn back and look at the tramp. He is probably my age. Change? I never carry 'change'. I open my wallet. There is nothing there but fifty-pound notes. I pull one out and hold it out by the corner. The man's eyes bulge.

'God bless you, sir,' he cries delightedly, and staggers away to spend the money on more booze. I look up and a star tumbles from the sky. I watch it and take it as a blessing.

I want desperately to go back to the apartment and get into bed beside her, but I won't. That will be a bad idea. She will be asleep and I will only wake her and want to get into that beautiful body. No, I want to do this properly. I will go back to my own apartment tonight and tomorrow I will meet her and tell her I am madly, madly in love with her.

I send her a text.

Meet me for breakfast outside the café? 9am. X

I am not asleep when his text comes through. I read his message and even though the very thought of breakfast makes me feel sick, I know I will go to him. Perhaps I will have some black coffee and pretend I am on a diet or something. I wonder where he is. Why has he not come to me? Has he begun to lose interest? So quickly? Alone and deeply sad, I go to sleep and sleep badly, tossing and turning. Eventually, when I do fall into a deep sleep, dawn is in the sky.

My alarm goes off at eight a.m.

I dress hurriedly in a long shirt and navy and white trousers. There is no bump yet, but it seems like a good idea to start dressing in loose attire. Carelessly I pull an Alice hair band on. It doesn't match my outfit, but I can't bring myself to care. Suddenly, I am wrecked by a wave of nausea. I lean against the mirror and fight it. I shouldn't have agreed to go, but I don't want to make him suspicious.

Downstairs, I wave to Mr. Nair and walk out of the building. The café is only down the street. As I walk my thoughts wander. What will become of me and the little life growing inside me? I put my head down and make a decision as I step onto the road. An urgent shout jars me out of my own little world.

'Watch out!'

My head jerks up. In that split second, I see Blake running towards me. He is no longer shouting. His face is ashen. As if in slow motion I turn and see a car speeding towards me. I should run, but my feet are rooted to the spot. Even far into the future I will remember how I saw everything so clearly it was like looking through a very clean glass. How Blake, his eyes full of desperate fear reached me and with both hands pushed me back with such force that I was thrown backwards and out of harm's way.

The car ploughs into him instead.

I lie on the ground and watch him flying in the air like a rag doll. He lands on the other side of the street. Even from my prone position I can see the stream of blood that starts running away from his head into the gray asphalt. I scramble up on my hands and knees and run to him screaming. He is lying on his front, but his head is turned in my direction.

'Are you all right?' he mumbles vaguely in the direction of my voice, but his eyes seem unable to focus.

'I'm fine,' I sob, and he closes his eyes and falls into some deep, dark place.

Someone calls the police and the ambulance is quick to arrive. They take him to the nearest emergency room, but I am keenly aware that his family will want him to be taken to the best hospital money can buy. I look through his mobile and find Marcus's number.

'Hello,' I say. My voice is strangely calm. It must be the shock, I guess.

'Who's this?' comes the suspicious reply.

'Blake has been in a road accident.' My voice shakes on the word accident. 'He's been taken to the Hospital of St John and St Elizabeth. I just thought you should know.'

'How bad is he?'

'It looks like a head injury, but there might be other internal things that I don't know about.'

'Are you at the hospital right now?'

'Yes.'

'Will you wait for me? I'll be right there.'

I sit on a chair feeling totally numb. There is blood on my wrists and hands. Blake's blood. Suspended inside my cloud of shock I stare at it blankly. Slowly as if in a daze I drag a finger through it. It feels sticky. *I'm not dreaming, this is really happening*, my brain says. I wipe my hand on my stained, torn navy and white trousers, take out my own mobile and call Billie.

Billie is quicker to arrive than Marcus. The sight of Billie's worried face hurrying towards me undoes me.

'Oh, Billie,' I sob. 'It was my fault. I wasn't looking where I was going. If he had not pushed me out of the way it would have been me that the car hit.'

'Banker boy threw himself under a car to save you?' Billie's eyebrows are almost in her hairline.

I stop crying, as I register what I have not with the shock. He is cold and unemotional. He hardly ever touches me unless he wants to have sex. Why?

'Why would he do that?' I whisper.

'People only do that for the people they love,' Billie says.

'He doesn't love me. If you knew what kind of relationship we have you'd never say that. He must have acted instinctively.'

Billie says nothing. Her eyes are on the door. 'Here comes big brother.'

I turn in the direction Billie is looking at and indeed, it is Blake's brother; he has the same superior air. He is standing at the door scanning the room. As soon as he spots us he comes over. His surprised eyes slide quickly over the spiders climbing on Billie's neck, but he only addresses me, as if he instinctively recognizes the type of woman his brother would be interested in.

'I'm Marcus. You must be the one who called me.'

'Yes.'

'Thank you. Where is my brother now?'

I point towards the desk. 'They won't tell me anything.'

'What happened?'

'He pushed me out of the way of a speeding car and took the hit himself.'

Marcus's face is incredulous. 'My brother did that?'

Tears begin to roll unchecked down my face. I feel like a complete fool crying in front of that disapproving stranger, but the tears refuse to stop.

He looks at my tears unemotionally. 'It will be the shock,' he says.

I nod through the tears.

He glances quickly at the two ladies behind the reception desk, obviously eager to talk to them. 'Look, if you give me your name and address, I will be happy to compensate you for what you have done.'

His words are like a slap. I take a shocked step away from him. I remember Blake saying, *we are not like you.* 'That won't be necessary,' I say.

An expression passes across his face. Irritation. He is irritated with me. 'Well, thank you for calling me, anyway.' He turns away from us and begins to walk towards the enquiries desk. Then he remembers, stops and comes back to me. 'Can I have my brother's phone back, please?'

Silently I put the phone into his outstretched hand.

'Thank you again for what you did for my brother,' he says awkwardly.

I nod and feel Billie's supportive hand come around my waist.

Marcus strides away. After the fear, the guilt, and the worry, the shock of his brother's utter rejection finishes me. I sag weakly against Billie.

'Fucking heartless, rude bastard. Fuck them and their pissy billions. They can keep it,' Billie says angrily. She leads me outside and hails a black cab. We get in and do not speak during the journey, but Billie tightly holds my hand in hers for the entire duration of the trip.

When we get out of the cab, I retch and am sick by the side of the road. An old biddy walking on the other side of the road stops to stare and Billie asks her if she has a tissue.

'Oh dear, oh dear,' she says, and crosses the road. She fishes a handkerchief from her handbag. 'What's the matter with the poor child?'

'She's pregnant,' Billie says.

My eyes swing around to Billie and Billie claps her hand over her mouth. 'Oh my God! You're pregnant, aren't you?'

'Can I have the handkerchief back?' the old biddy whines plaintively.

Billie takes the soiled cloth from me and ungratefully stuffs it into the woman's hand. 'Thanks, love. You want to stock up on tissues in future. More hygienic.'

The woman leaves with a sniff and Billie turns to me. 'Why didn't you tell me?'

'I just found out myself. Besides, I can't keep it.'

Billie's eyes open wide. 'What?'

I blink back the tears. 'It's in my contract. If I don't terminate I will forfeit all rights to it. I'm not going to give up my baby to that cold bunch.'

Billie's eyes flash. 'They can't do that.'

'They can, Bill. The way they feel about crushing us is the way you feel about killing a row of ants heading towards your jam jar.'

'Who do they think you are? Fucking Oliver Twist? Please, sir, can I have some more, sir? You know what? I haven't used any of the money that you gave me. Let's give that back to them and work out some plan where we pay the rest back with interest.'

I shake my head tiredly. 'Oh, Bill, they don't want the money back. It's all about their precious bloodline. The purity of the great Barrington line must be safeguarded at all costs. And any bastard children must go back to the Barrington care. They don't trust the likes of us to bring up children properly.'

Billie looks as though she is about to go into one. A very long and loud rant.

'Not now, Bill. Please. I just want to go somewhere I can sit.'

Billie holds out her hand. 'Come. I'll take you home.'

'I don't want my mum to know.'

'It's OK, we'll go to mine and you can clean up there. We don't have to tell anyone.'

'Remember when you said you didn't know whether you would share your lottery money with me if you ever did win?'

'Yeah.'

'Now you know, don't you?'

Billie smiles sadly. 'Yeah, now I know.'

Thirty

Victoria Jane Montgomery

I walk up to the nurse.

'Good afternoon, Miss Montgomery.'

'Good afternoon. How is he today?'

'He seems better. I just looked in on him a few minutes ago and he was asleep, but he was conscious for a few minutes this morning, and seemed desperate to know if someone called Lana was all right? It would be good to reassure him that she is all right.'

I can't stop the pure rush of shock that invades my body. I shutter my beautiful green eyes and smile. 'If he asks again, tell him not to worry about her. She is fine.'

'I certainly will, Miss Montgomery.'

I nod politely and walk down the corridor. My heart feels as if it is breaking. I enter his room and shut the door behind me. It is quiet and full of flowers. My eyes move to his face. His eyes are closed and he is very still. I walk up to his bed and stand looking down on him. He looks so helpless and pale under his dark tan that I feel an odd rush of emotion inside me. I know it is very dull of me, but I love this man. I can't even care that my friends call me Sticky Vicky behind my back.

'Oh, darling,' I whisper. 'What a perfectly awful fright you gave me.'

I take his big hand in my small dainty ones and caress the inside of his wrist. Ever since I met him at my garden party when I was ten years old I have loved him.

'I'm going to marry that boy,' I told my father.

My father threw back his head and laughed, but his eyes had gleamed strangely. He approved. And over the years he had quietly encouraged my total dedication to 'that boy'. When the families decided that it would be a perfect match I celebrated quietly. While Blake indulged in his meaningless affairs and liaisons I laid low. Of course, my father did not and would never know about the drunken one-night stands.

Those don't count.

I let my finger trace a vein. There is nothing I will not do for this man. I bend down and kiss that straight mouth—his lips feel cool and dry—and I remember that other time I pressed my lips to his. Then, he was fifteen. He wiped his lips with the back of his hand and looked at me scornfully. 'You're just a baby. Lip kisses are for grown-ups,' he chided.

Very gently I push back a piece of hair that has strayed onto his forehead and smooth it down. I know he is not in love with me. But I can live with that. I will take him on any terms. I want his seed in me. I want to see him in my children's faces. I want to watch the gray appear in his temples. I want to sit out in my father's French seaside villa when we are both old and gray watching the sunset together. But for now a fond look, an affectionate smile, a caring touch from him will be enough for me.

For a long time, I am content to simply sit with my cheek pressed against his hand. Eventually, there is a noise at the door and Marcus enters. He stands awkwardly in the middle of the room for a moment.

'Hello, Marcus,' I greet with a smile.

'How are you?' he says politely, and coming over to me, lightly kisses both my cheeks.

'I'm fine, thank you.'

He nods distractedly. 'The nurse told me he regained consciousness for a short while. Were you here? Did he say anything?'

I shake my head. 'I wasn't here.' He's never going to know about the slut Blake has installed in a penthouse in St John's Wood. 'How did it happen?' I ask instead.

'I don't know…exactly,' he says evasively, and moves to the other side of the bed.

Ah, so he knows something that he doesn't want me to know. Blake's accident must have something to do with that whore! I feel a new clutch of pain in my heart. All this while I thought it was not serious, that it was a strictly sex thing. I saw the contract, after all. The pain is so strong I feel like howling.

'I guess I'll come back in the evening,' I say. My voice sounds strange.

I close the door and quickly walk along the corridor. I hate the smell of hospitals. It always reminds me of the many months my grandmother spent in her sick bed before she died. As I round the corner I come to a dead stop. The nurse at the desk is talking to Blake's tart and a ghoul-like creature covered in tattoos.

Anger bubbles inside me. These low class people. How dare they? How dare they show up at this hospital where my father could very well come to? The cheek of it. I hear the nurse very firmly enforce the instructions I left.

'I'm sorry but I have very strict instructions not to let anyone in, but the family members on this list.'

For a while it appears as if the ghoul would fight it out but Blake's tart takes a step back and the ghoul says loudly, 'You're right, Lana, lets leave these stuck-up, la di da shits to get on with it.' Then she grabs the slut's hand and pulls her away. They do not see me.

Now I know. Something has to be done.

Thirty one

Lana Bloom

The doorbell rings and I start with surprise. There is always somebody at my mother's door wanting to borrow a hairdryer, a pen, red lipstick, a sparkly handbag, or something. But here? None of my friends are allowed to visit. Besides…unannounced by Mr. Nair?

I walk to the door and look out of the eyehole.

There is a woman standing outside. She looks to be in her early twenties. Her skin is very good, her lipstick is pale, and her glossy brown hair is held back by a black velvet band. She is dressed as if she is going to a lawn party. In an elegant linen dress and black pearls.

I know who she is.

I open the door and, oddly, note that I would never have thought to combine black pearls with such an outfit. From every pore of her flawless skin she exudes good breeding and finishing school class. She is pure style.

You can live in a fine home, wear the right clothes and even go to the right parties but you will never be one of us, her very being seems to say.

Her mouth curves into a smile. 'Hello, I'm Victoria. May I come in?'

I cannot stop staring at her. So this is the woman that Blake is going to marry. This is the woman who will have his babies and live with him.

'Please,' she says.

I open the door wider and stand back.

She enters and looks around the room curiously, but refrains from commenting. I precede her into the living room and turn around to face her.

'You are prettier in real life.'

I don't know if I should acknowledge the compliment. In the end I don't. It is not sincere.

'May I sit?'

I nod and she perches at the end of a sofa. Her movements are all dainty. She transfers the small pink purse from her hand to her lap and crosses her slim ankles.

Then she looks at me and smiles again. 'Will you sit too?'

I flush and sit. This is not the woman's territory and yet it seems she has somehow taken charge.

'I know you are shocked to see me here and even more shocked to see that I neither hate nor feel angry with you. You see, our ways are different. You'll probably never understand so I won't try to explain too much. Suffice to say that I don't think it is ideal, especially from the women's point of view, but I am willing to concede that men must sow their wild oats before they settle down, so I allow it.'

My lips part.

'I know what you are hoping for.'

I make a strangled sound in my throat. 'Really?'

'You are hoping for exactly the same thing that every woman who has signed one of these sordid agreements and who then falls in love dreams of. You want Blake to fall in love with you and marry you.'

I cannot help it, wild color rushes up my throat.

Her eyes flash. 'But he never will. Men like him have been taught since they were knee high how to take, how to have their cake and eat it in every situation.'

She stops to make a little face.

'Marrying you or staying with you will not be that. This agreement with you, until he gets bored, and then, marrying me, will be the option most desirable to our men. And that is what Blake will do too.' She looks at me innocently. 'Has he in any way suggested more than this arrangement? Perhaps given you hope for a different future with him?'

Woodenly, I shake my head.

She smiles with great satisfaction. 'I thought so. You see, the most important thing for us is to secure the right bloodlines for our children and ensure our wealth is not dissipated away into careless hands. Blake knows where his loyalties lie. Consequently, I fear nothing from you. If anything, I feel sorry for you and want to be fair to you. I can see that you are in love with him, and in the end, you will be left with nothing more than a broken heart.'

I had been staring at the carpet but at her words my head snaps up. 'What do you want?' I blurt out.

'Well, I guess I might as well come to the point. Nobody knows I'm here and Mummy would scream blue murder if she knew I was.'

'So why are you here?'

'I know your contract will expire in six weeks.'

'How do you know that?'

'I have my ways. It is not important to our discussion today. Strange as it may seem, I am now your only friend.'

I cannot imagine a scenario where this condescending, utterly self-obsessed woman could be my friend. Let alone my only friend.

'What is important to you must be that you are adequately compensated at the end of your time here.' She pauses meaningfully. 'Of course, there is a possibility that Blake will extend or renew the contract for another three months. Then again there is the distinct possibility he will not. I am here to offer you a hundred thousand pounds for you to leave…not at the end of the contract, but today. Since there is no punitive action allowed in your contract if you end it earlier than its term you are within your rights to do so.'

I look at her with shock. I glanced through the contract so fast I did not even register that clause. Yet this woman has perused the contract carefully and is here to bargain with me.

'I will increase the amount to two hundred thousand pounds if you will leave the country. No note. No goodbyes. No explanations. Just gone.'

No note. No goodbyes. No explanations. Just gone.

Wow! I look at the young woman who sits so brazenly before me and feel a bubble of hysterical laughter forming in my throat. Unsteadily, I stand up and walk to the glass wall. Far below there are small children playing with a dog in the park. With my back to the woman, I close my eyes and try to think, but my mind is blank with horror.

'Did you think that the billionaire's son would marry the poor girl from the council estate?'

I flush. 'Of course not.'

Except for that once when I tasted my name joined with his, I have not really thought that. Always from the start it has been made clear to me that it is a purely temporary arrangement based solely on sex. He has only ever wanted me for one thing and he has been brutally honest about it. There have been no protestations of love or flowery words. Just an animal craving for my skin.

As if the woman opposite me has heard my thoughts she remarks quietly, 'Cravings go away.'

'Please leave,' I say, without turning around. I am glad to hear that my voice is firm and strong. I hear the woman stand.

'You will regret this one day,' she says. There is no malice in her voice. She is simply stating a fact. Unemotionally. 'If you change your mind, my card is on the table. Please don't mention my visit to anyone.'

I nod.

After I hear the door close I stand before a beautiful gilded mirror and look at myself. How changed I am. My eyes are full of pain. There are bruises under my eyes where there were none. My hand moves to my belly. Soon I will be showing. I think of the woman. At the heartless determination hidden within the beautiful exterior. Between them, they will kill the life growing inside me. I love Blake with all my heart, but for him I am only a wild oat.

I must stop being selfish and think only of the little one inside me now. Secure his or her future. I press my hand to my mouth and stop the cry that threatens to escape. Tears are streaming down my face. I wipe them with the backs of my hands and run out of the door. Victoria is waiting by the lift. She turns to look at me and for that one pure moment, I understand how murderers feel. I want to steal this woman's heartbeat, take her life and the man that fate has so arbitrarily assigned to her.

'I'll take...' my voice breaks. I force myself to spit out the words,...'the money.'

She smiles. It is not the smile of a victor. It is not malicious. It is not unkind. Neither is it pitying nor condescending. It is simply the lucky smile of a woman who has never been refused anything her heart desires.

Thirty two

Victoria Jane Montgomery

I am Victoria Jane Montgomery, daughter of the fourth Earl of Hardwicke and I will have my way.

I enter the large conservatory built on the east wall of my father's home. In my opinion, it is the most beautiful part of the house, with its old Victorian stained glass and its profusion of citrus trees, tropical palms, and orchids. When I was younger there was even a banana tree. But Geoffrey died some years ago and this new gardener has other ideas, newer ideas.

My mother, she has pink cheeks, soft blue eyes and a small pink mouth, is reading a book. Another cheap period romance with a swashbuckling man clutching a buxom woman with flowing hair on the cover. I have never understood why a woman of her age should read romances. Surely, the instinct for romance dies when one reaches a certain age. In fact, I have never understood the allure of romances. They bore me. You see, I have the real thing in my life. I have Blake, all six feet three inches of him.

And all I have to do to make my toes clench is to think of him. But when I think of him with that hussy, my stomach actually knots and I have to stop myself from doing the bitch bodily harm. In fact, in a dream I once had I tore her eyes out. The feeling of hate is so strong that sometimes I have to clench my hands, so hard my nails bite into my flesh and leave half moon marks.

My mother looks up from her book. 'Oh, daahling. Have you just come from the hospital? How is Blake doing?'

Her King Charles, Suki, jumps dementedly at my feet. I pick it up and, tickling the fur next to its pink crystal-studded collar, sit on a chair opposite my mother.

'He hasn't come around yet,' I say, as the dog tries to lick my mouth.

'Oh dear, what are the doctors saying?'

'It's a matter of time. The swelling needs to go down. They expect to be able to operate tomorrow.'

'I'm sorry, my dear.'

'Actually, Mummy, I've come to talk to you about a different matter.'

'Oh?' My mother puts her book down.

'Well, it is about Blake, but it's not about his accident, well maybe it is, a little bit. Anyway, I found out that Blake has a mistress.'

'Oh,' my mother says again. I bite my lip. It is a blow to my pride to tell my mother this.

'I went to the apartment where he keeps her and paid her to leave the country and never see him again. Her mother is Iranian or something, and I suggested she live there for a while until everything blows over.'

The foolish look suddenly drops from my mother's eyes and her voice loses that simpering softness that I grew up with. My mouth drops open in shock. In that moment I realize I have never really known my mother. This woman is nobody's fool.

'You have taken a huge and unnecessary risk by doing that. These types of women will grow in such soil as ours and wither quickly, but when you force one out by the roots the way you have done, they leave a mark, an ugly scar that some men will mistake for a lost love.'

The wisdom in my mother's words makes undeniable sense and I look at her worriedly. 'But he took her to the Craft ball!'

She looks at me with narrowed eyes. 'How do you know that?'

I look away and gently lower Suki to the ground.

My mother sighs and throws an imperial mint to the floor. Immediately Suki catches it in her mouth and crunches it. 'You've had him followed. You are playing a dangerous game, Victoria. What does she look like?'

'A slut.'

My mother looks at me steadily.

'All right, she's very beautiful and young,' I spit out.

'But dirt poor?'

'Poorer than dirt.'

'Oh dear. Perhaps you did the right thing then.'

'But what do I do now?'

'Nothing much. Persuade your father to talk to Blake and take the blame for paying the girl off. It will appear less sordid if such a thing is done by a father to protect his daughter's interest. You must remain spotless. Go and see your father. He is in the study. He never could resist a tear or two from you.'

I stand and my mother says, 'You do know that this will not be the last woman that will come into your life, don't you?'

'Yes.'

'Are you sure you want this life?'

I did not hesitate. 'Yes.'

My mother nods sadly. 'Remember this. I married beneath me. So will you. All women do.'

I stare at her in shock.

'Well, run along then, daahling,' she simpers and picks up her lurid novel.

Thirty three

Lana Bloom

The first person I call is Jack. He answers on the fifth ring just as I am about to give up.

'What is it?' he asks, instantly alert.

'Oh, Jack,' I cry.

'Where are you?'

'Going to Mum's.'

'I'll meet you there.'

'You don't have to meet me there, Jack. I only wanted to hear your voice.'

'What happened?'

'Nothing.' But my voice breaks.

'Fuck nothing. What happened?'

'I have to leave. I'm taking Mum back to Iran.'

'What?'

'Just for a year.'

'I'm coming over.'

'Please don't, Jack. I was feeling weak, but I'm all right now. Funny, just hearing your voice did it. I know now what I have to do. I'll email you when I get settled. It's a bit primitive over there, so it might take a bit of time, but you and Billie will be the first people I write to.'

'Don't you want to see me before you go?'

'I'll be gone by the time you get here. Someone else is making the arrangements and they don't mess about. I'm afraid I kinda jumped from the frying pan into the fire, but I think it will be OK when I get to Iran.'

'What about Blake?'

'He's history. He must never know where I am.'

'Has he hurt you?'

'No. He's still unconscious in hospital.'

'You're not going of your own free will, are you?'

'No, but it is for the best. I've got to go now, Jack. I will write as soon as I can.'

'Goodbye, Lana.'

'Goodbye, darling Jack.'

Thirty four

Victoria Montgomery

It is a rich room in which I find my father. He is sitting in a large armchair reading the newspapers, and his favorite foxhound, Sergeant is curled up on a rug at his feet. At my entrance, Sergeant does no more than swivel his mournful eyes in my direction and wave the tip of his thirteen-year-old tail.

'Daddy.'

My father tilts his head so his washed out blue eyes can peer over the tops of his glasses. 'Hello, pet,' he welcomes genially.

'Daddy, I've done something rather dreadful.' I clasp my hands in front of me

He lowers his paper and narrows his eyes. It is amazing how different his eyes now appear.

'Sit down,' he orders.

I walk over to the chair opposite him, making sure my face is troubled and unhappy.

'Well?' he prompts.

I look down and twist a black pearl on my bracelet. 'I found out that Blake was keeping a woman. A horrible woman from a council estate.' I stand suddenly and move a few feet away. 'He was paying her.'

My father wisely says nothing. I glance at him. He is watching me carefully.

'Anyway, I went to see her and it was awful. Just awful. Ghastly woman. There she was in all the designer gear that he had bought her, and she was so arrogant about it too. She challenged me to take him away from her. I was so desperate I offered her money to leave him.' I turn around and look him directly in the eye.

My father's face is deliberately expressionless. 'Did she agree?'

My voice is instantly hard and cold. 'Of course. I had Martin draw up the papers and I transferred the money from my Gibraltar account. I've checked and she's gone. Left the country.'

'It appears you've taken care of your little problem. What do you want me to do?'

'Daddy, I love Blake, he is a good, strong man, and I know that once we are married he will be a good husband and a fine father. I can forgive him for this little indiscretion.'

My father nods carefully.

'But I know that he will never forgive me for interfering with his affairs if he finds out it was I who offered her the money. Mummy had a brilliant idea. She thought it would be better if you tell him that it was you who offered her the money. Surely, he will be able to see what a little tramp she is to leave him while he is still in hospital.'

'But that will surely ruin my relationship with him.'

'Does it really matter? You will still be his father-in-law and in time he will come to recognize that you did it for his own good.'

'You are certain you want this man?'

'I have never been more certain of anything in my life.'

He turns away from me and looks out of the window. 'Do you have a copy of her signature?'

'Yes.'

He nods. 'Of course, the contract.' A thought occurs to him. 'What about a sample of her writing?'

'Yes.'

He raises a bushy, enquiring eyebrow.

'I have a copy of her application form from the temporary agency she used to work at.'

He smiles. I can tell he is impressed. 'Give them both to me. I will work something out with Jason.' I have never met Jason, but I know of him. He is a master forger.

'Thank you, Daddy,' I say and running up to him snuggle my softly perfumed cheek against his. My father's arm comes around my shoulder and he gives me an affectionate squeeze.

'Oh, my pretty, pretty little viper—what that man doesn't know about you!'

I move away from him and look up into his eyes.

'Daddy?'

'Yes, darling.'

'Is it very wrong what I have done?'

'You should have left it alone, Victoria. He is a man and men, my dear, have needs, but these needs do go away.'

'He took her to the Crafts ball.'

My father's eyes narrow to slits with disapproval. Immediately I feel bad that I told him that. I want my father to think well of Blake.

'He's a good man, Daddy. He's just a bit lost. She has bewitched him. He has never done anything like this before.'

My father says nothing but it is obvious he is unimpressed.

I cannot leave it alone. 'Are you angry with me, Daddy?' I ask, my eyes misting over.

'Of course not. You did what you thought was best, but there is a very important lesson that a woman can learn from a dog. When a dog finds another dog's scent on his master, he does not panic, feel threatened or hurl abuse, but merely finds it interesting. If you can cultivate that habit you will have a very happy marriage.'

Hugo Montgomery

When my daughter leaves, I look out of the window at the rolling green fields of my estate and the beautiful Van Gogh clouds in the sky. Shame Victoria had not been born a boy. I could have used her at the helm of the family instead of being a tool of consolidation.

I have known about Blake's woman. Seen photos of them together. Something about the pictures make me worry that this might not be the end of the matter. Still, my daughter is an intelligent, cunning little viper. And to date there is nothing she has wanted that has eluded her.

To be continued...

About the Author

Hey **you**,

Thank you for choosing and reading Owned. It is my first attempt at Contemporary Romance, and I have to say I simply *loved* writing it, especially the steamy scenes!

Book 2 is written through Lana's eyes.

Once again, fate has dropped her at Blake's feet, but he is no longer the man who upgraded her mother to first class, took care of her when she was as sick as a dog, or risked his own life to save hers. He is a cold-eyed, vengeful stranger who demands that she finish the term of the contract.

He is owed 42 days, and he will have it.

See you inside the pages of Forty 2 Days. Until then, go kiss a good-looking stranger. ☺

xx*Georgia*

Feel like saying hello or just want to know what the totally delectable Blake looks like?
https://www.facebook.com/georgia.lecarre